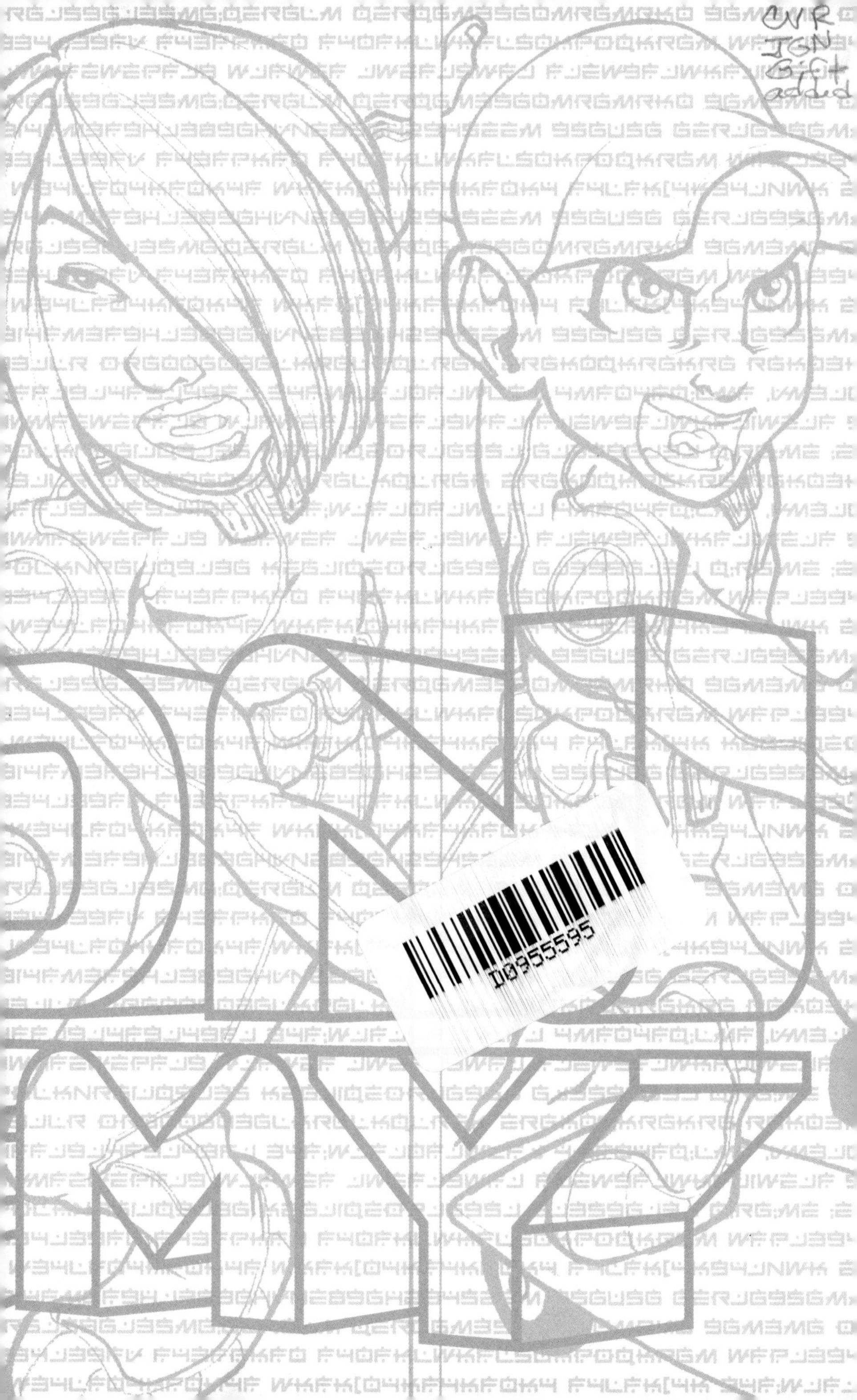

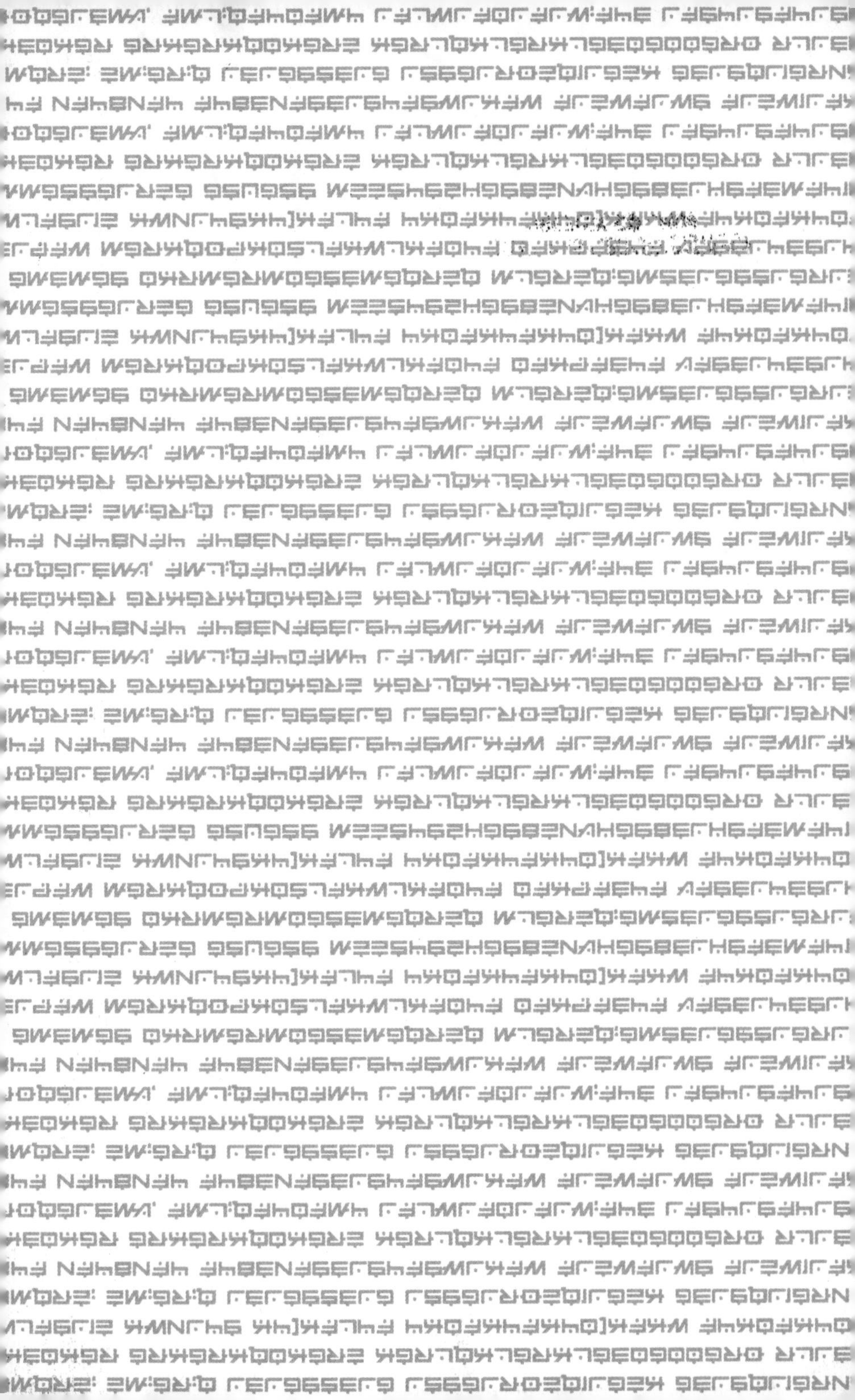

STONE ARCH BOOKS
MINNEAPOLIS   SAN DIEGO

HIGH PLAINS LIBRARY DISTRICT
GREELEY, CO 80634

《《《 ACCESS GRANTED 》》》

FILE NO.

SHADOW CELL SCAM

BY CHRIS EVERHEART
ILLUSTRATED BY ARCANA STUDIO

Recon Academy is published by Stone Arch Books
151 Good Counsel Drive, P.O. Box 669
Mankato, Minnesota 56002
www.stonearchbooks.com

Library of Congress Cataloging-in-Publication Data

Everheart, Chris.
  Shadow Cell Scam / by Chris Everheart; illustrated by Arcana Studio.
    p. cm. — (Recon Academy)
  ISBN 978-1-4342-1166-8 (library binding)
  ISBN 978-1-4342-1383-9 (pbk.)
  1. Graphic novels. [1. Graphic novels. 2. Terrorism—Fiction.] I. Arcana
Studio. II. Title.
  PZ7.7.E94Shc 2009
  [Fic]—dc22
                                                                  2008032074

Summary: The U.S. Navy is launching a secret spy satellite near Seaside
High School. However, the Recon Academy is too distracted to provide
their usual security. Each team member has just received a brand new laptop
computer — for free! The deal is too good to be true. When the machines
go haywire, the team must scramble to save themselves and the satellite.

Designer: Bob Lentz
Series Editor: Donnie Lemke
Series Concept: Michael Dahl, Brann Garvey, Heather Kindseth,
    Donnie Lemke

1 2 3 4 5 6 7 8 9 10 11 12 13 14 15 09

Printed in the United States of America

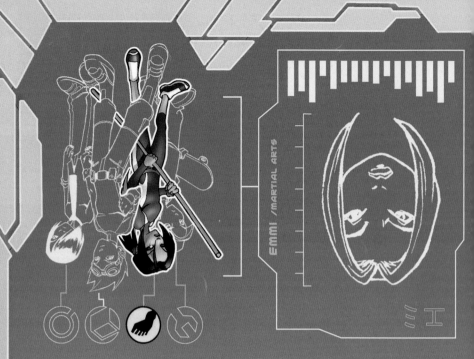

EMMI / MARTIAL ARTS

⟩ TABLE OF CONTENTS

⟩⟩⟩ ENTER

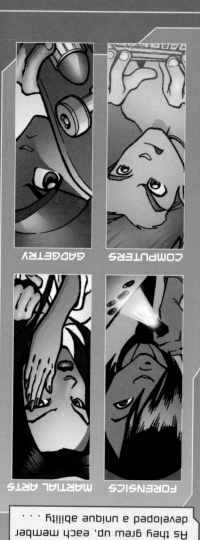

GADGETRY

COMPUTERS

MARTIAL ARTS

FORENSICS

As they grew up, each member developed a unique ability . . .

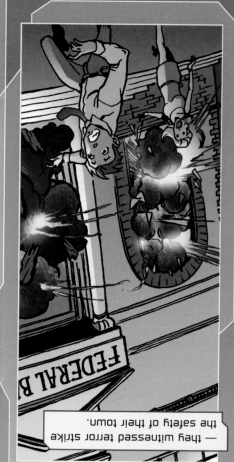

— they witnessed terror strike the safety of their town.

FEDERAL B...

Born into a world of rising threat —

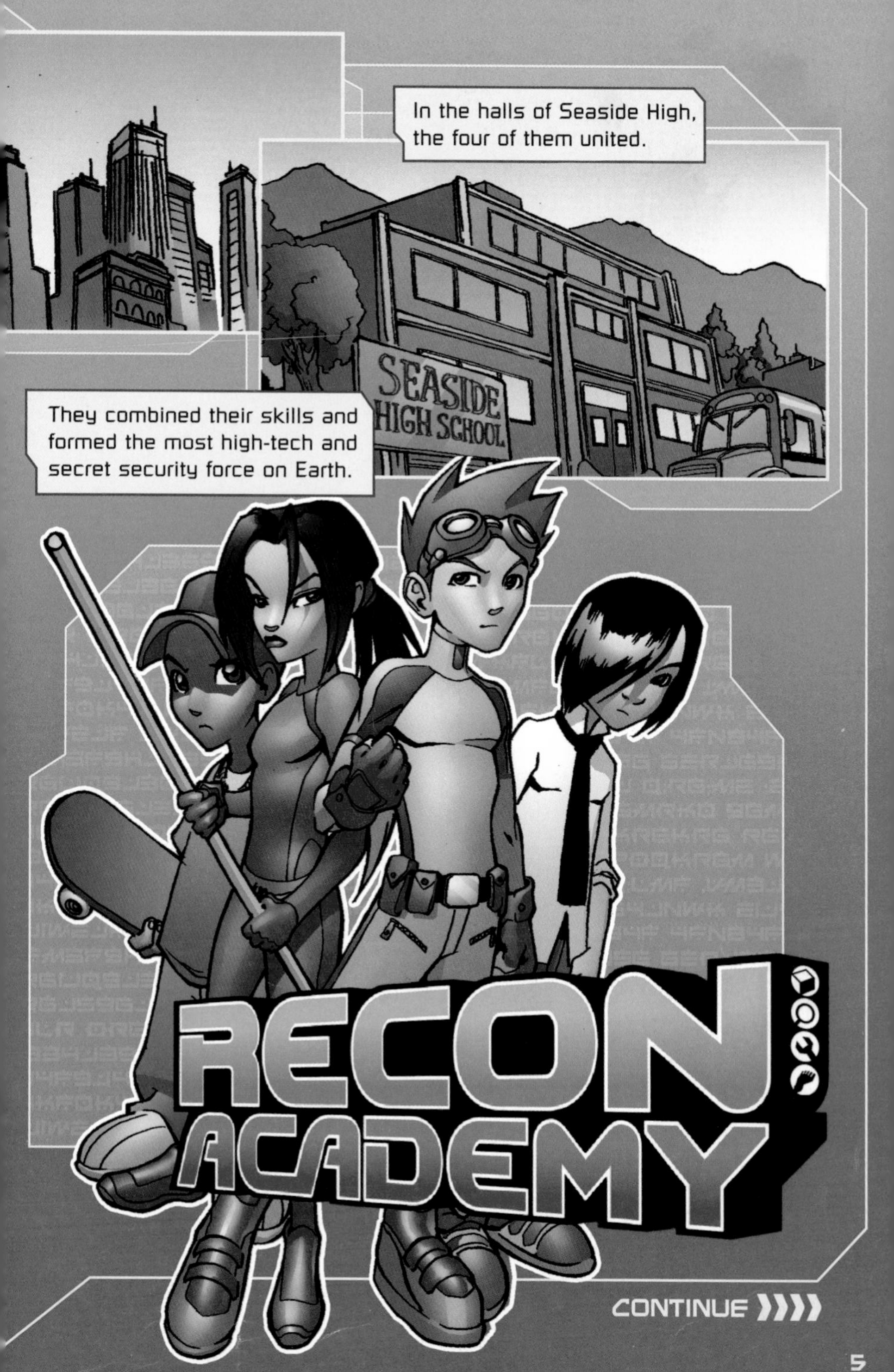
In the halls of Seaside High, the four of them united.
SEASIDE HIGH SCHOOL
They combined their skills and formed the most high-tech and secret security force on Earth.
RECON ACADEMY
CONTINUE

EMMI
MARTIAL ARTS

1992
129109
109201
1
89
68289
9283
628289
293829
12871B

ACCESS GRANTED »»

SECTION 1

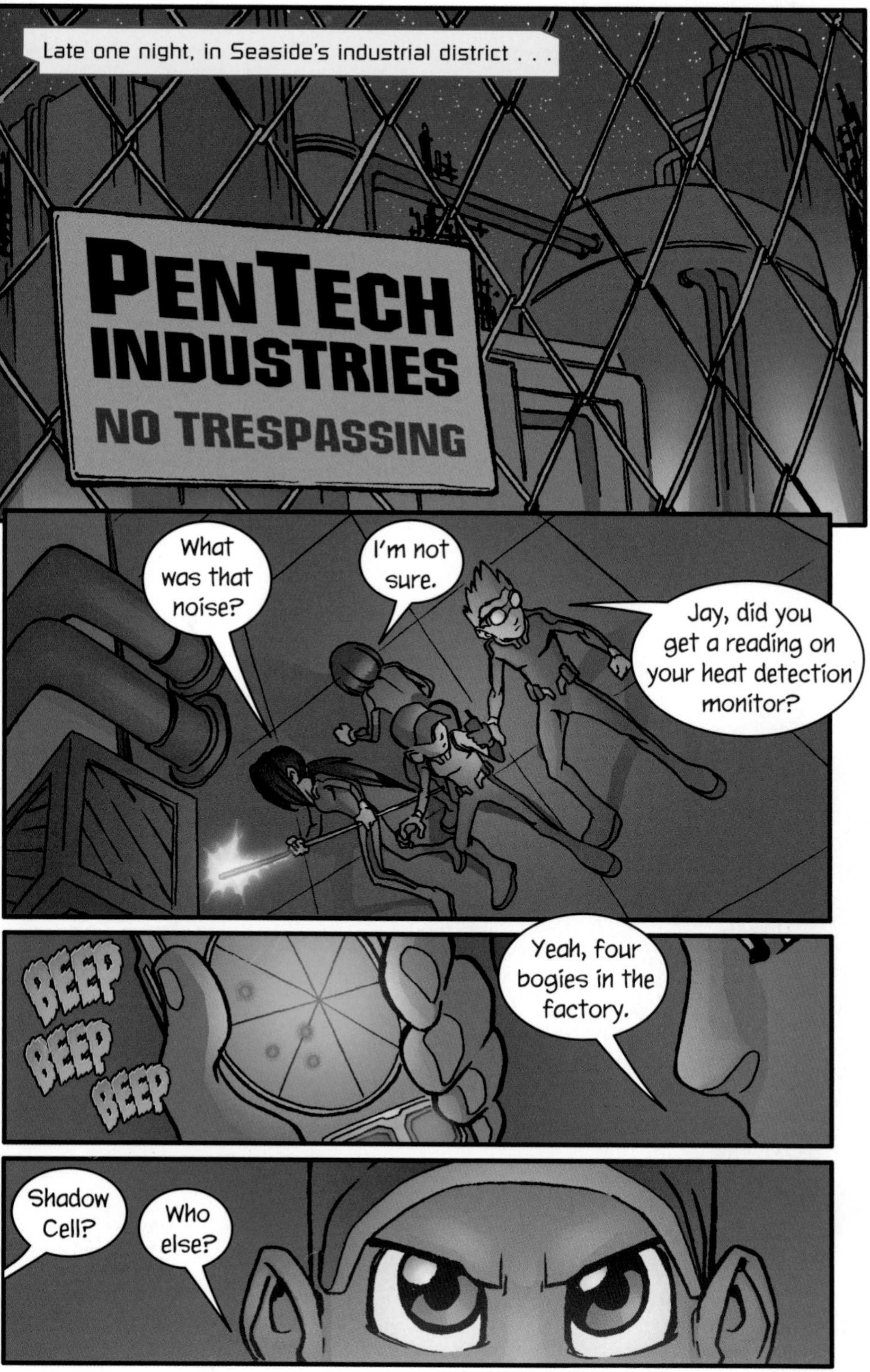
Late one night, in Seaside's industrial district . . .
PENTECH INDUSTRIES
NO TRESPASSING
What was that noise?
I'm not sure.
Jay, did you get a reading on your heat detection monitor?
BEEP
BEEP
BEEP
Yeah, four bogies in the factory.
Shadow Cell?
Who else?

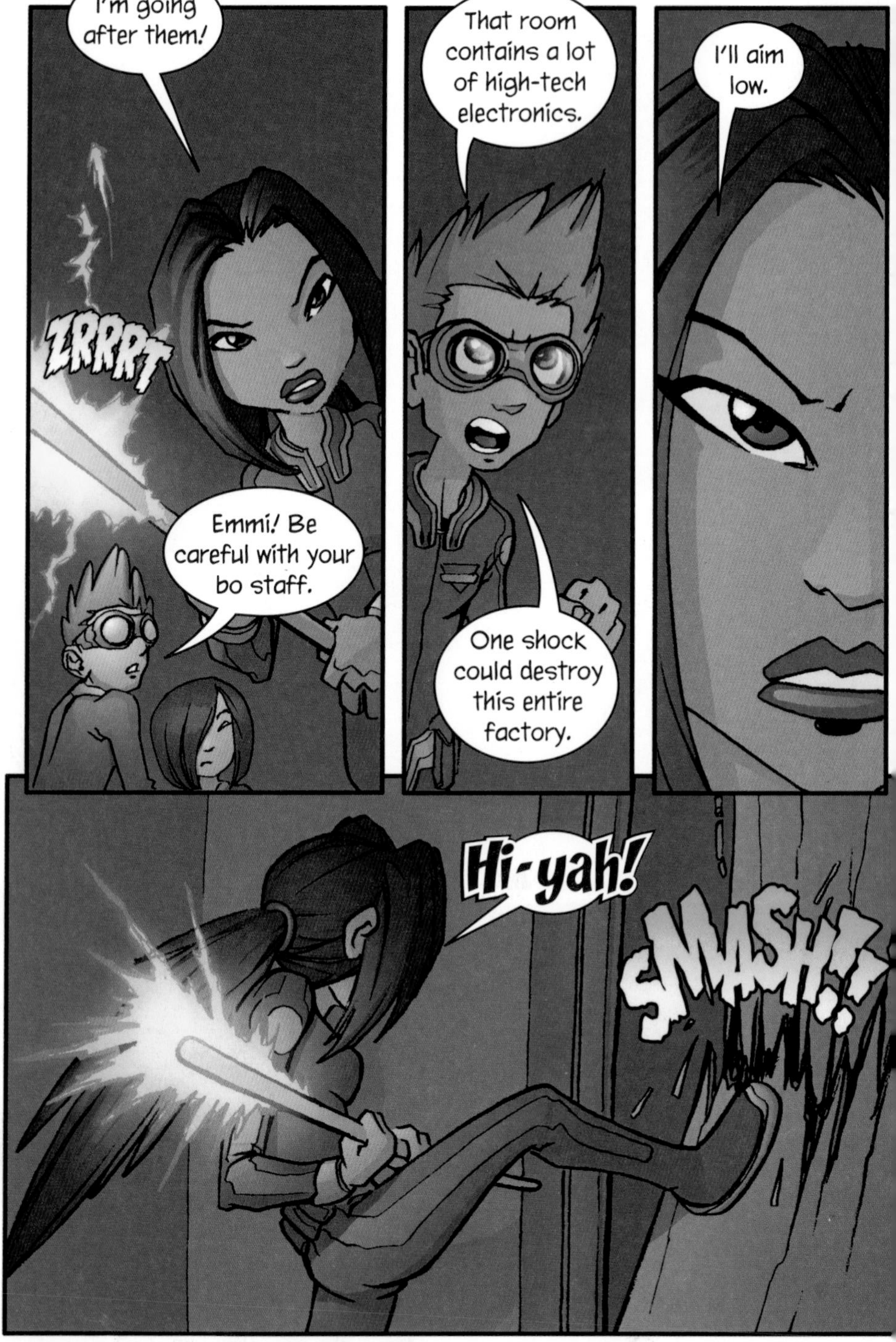
I'm going after them!
ZRRRT
Emmi! Be careful with your bo staff.
That room contains a lot of high-tech electronics.
One shock could destroy this entire factory.
I'll aim low.
Hi-yah!
SMASH!!

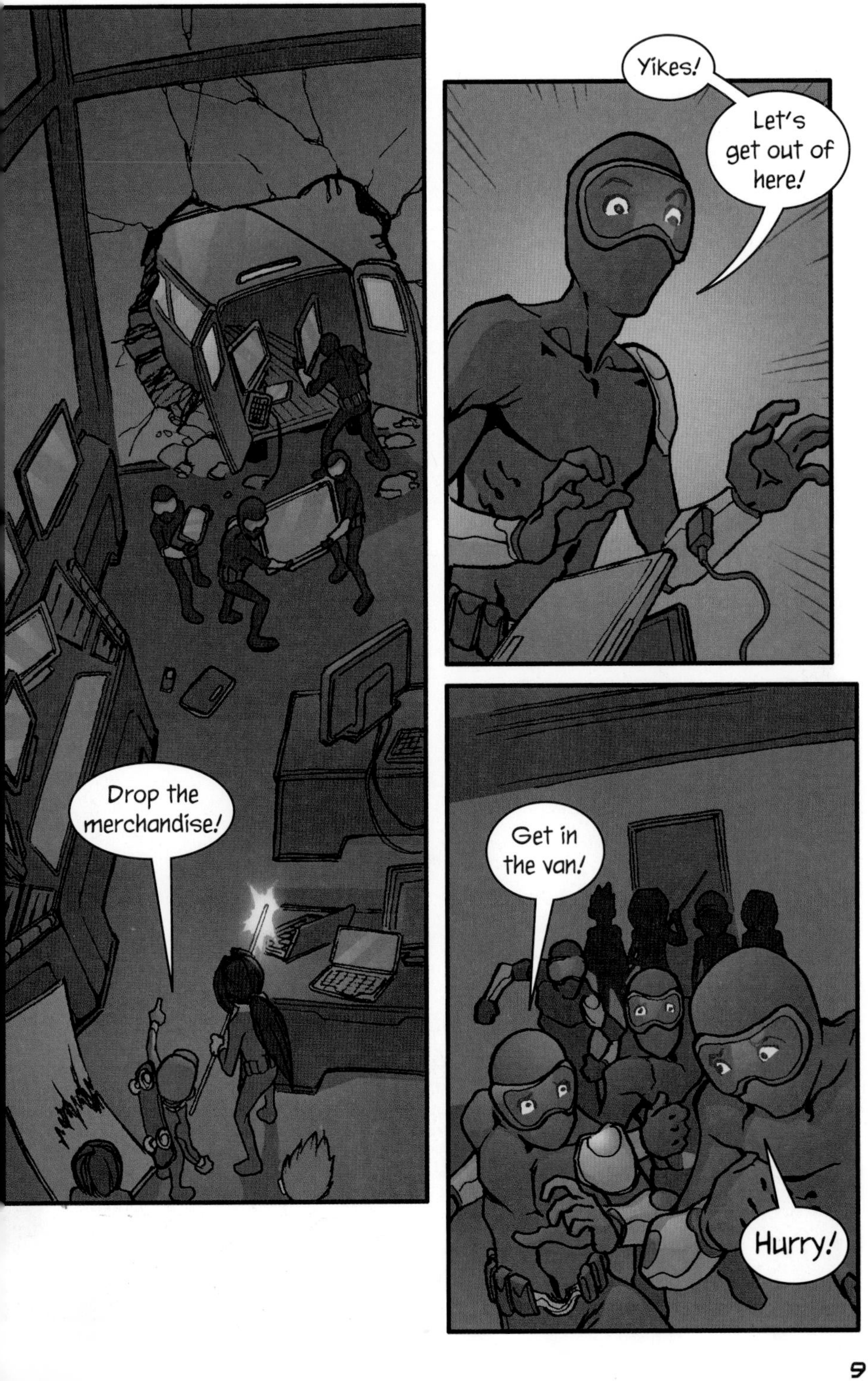
Drop the merchandise!
Yikes!
Let's get out of here!
Get in the van!
Hurry!

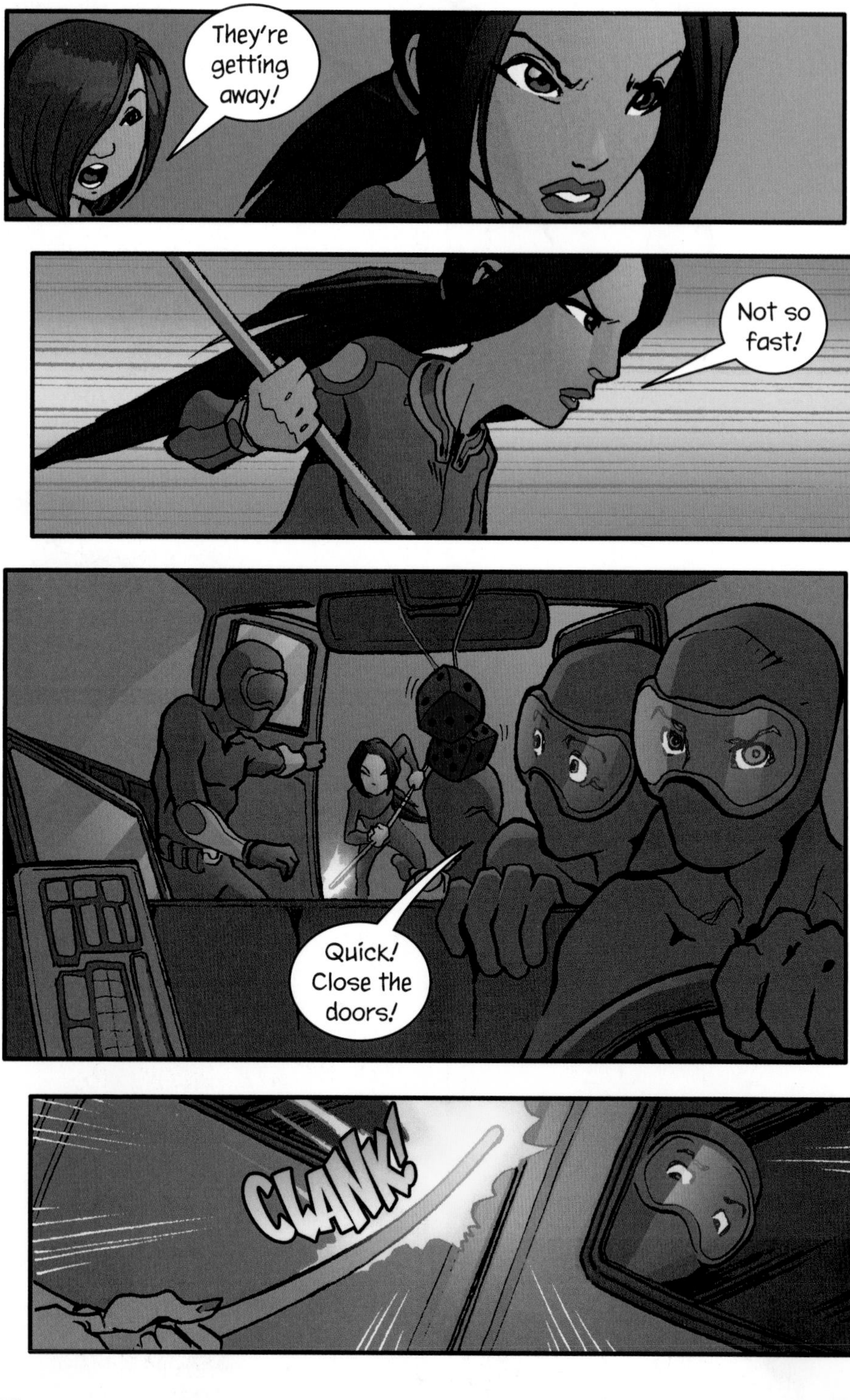
They're getting away!
Not so fast!
Quick! Close the doors!
CLANK!

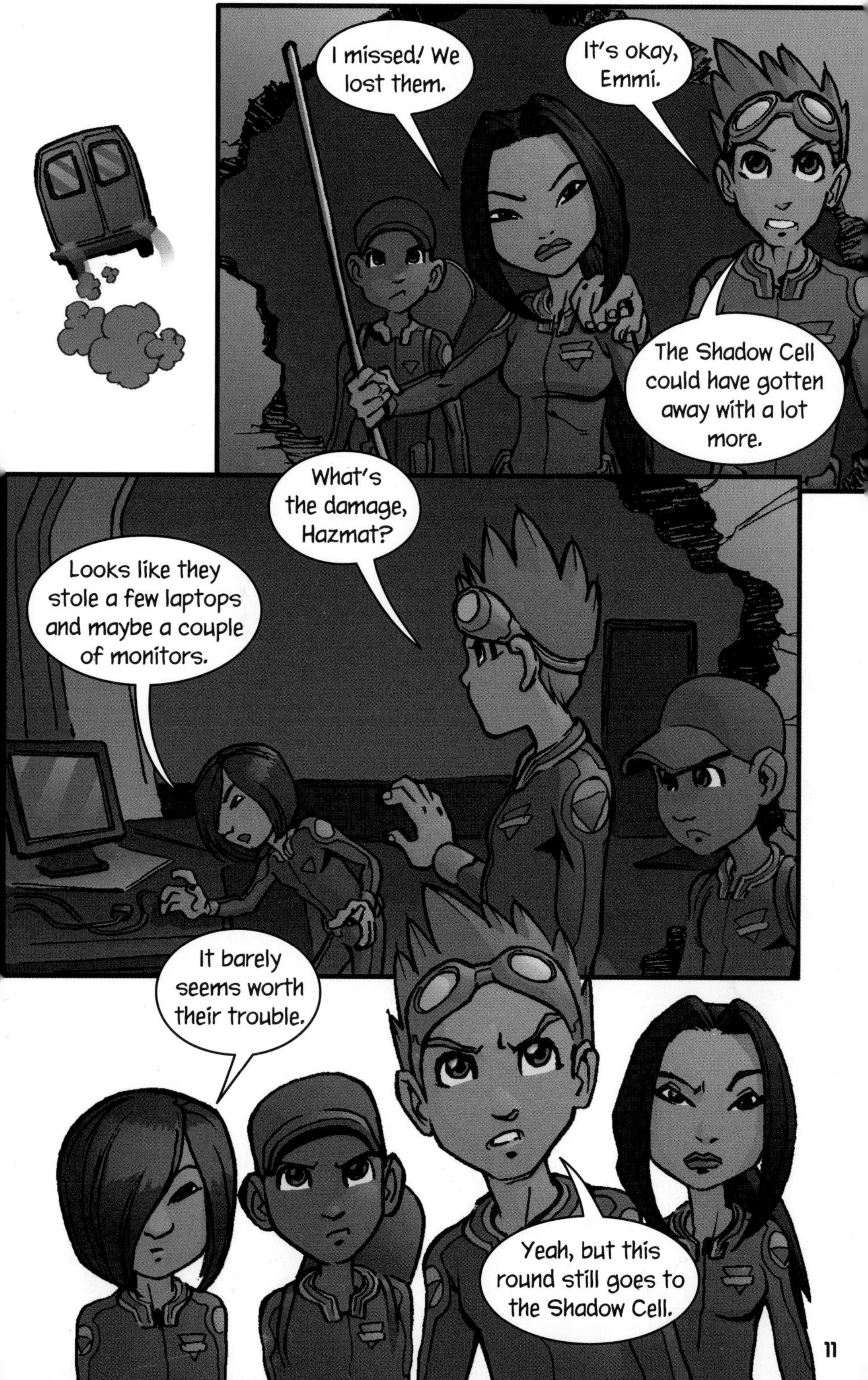
I missed! We lost them.
It's okay, Emmi.
The Shadow Cell could have gotten away with a lot more.
What's the damage, Hazmat?
Looks like they stole a few laptops and maybe a couple of monitors.
It barely seems worth their trouble.
Yeah, but this round still goes to the Shadow Cell.

EMMI
MARTIAL ARTS

128718
293829
8283
28986
89
1
109201
190261
1992

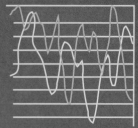

ACCESS GRANTED ﹥﹥﹥

2

SECTION

FILE NO.
143578

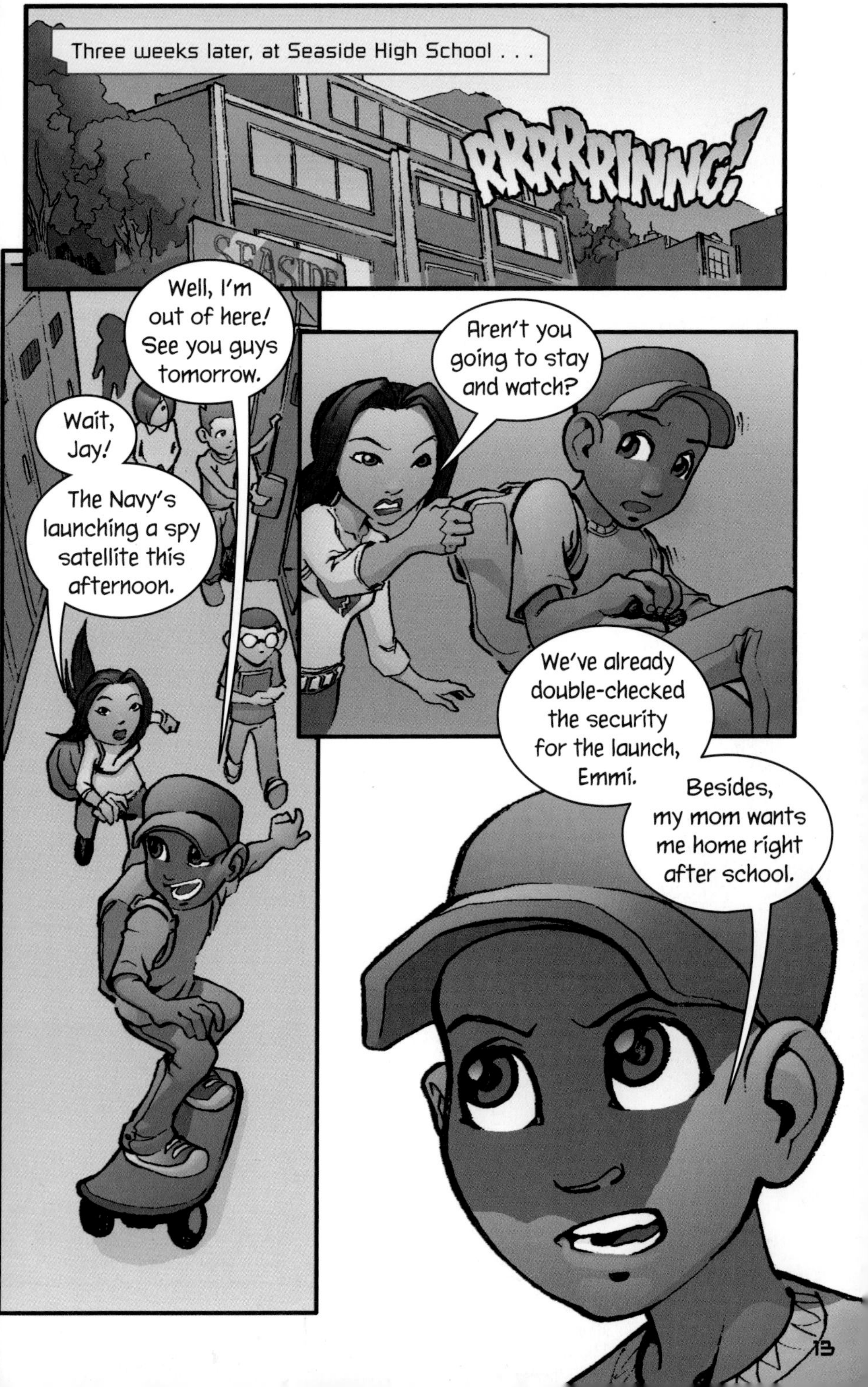
Three weeks later, at Seaside High School . . .
RRRRRINNG!
SEASIDE
Well, I'm out of here! See you guys tomorrow.
Wait, Jay!
The Navy's launching a spy satellite this afternoon.
Aren't you going to stay and watch?
We've already double-checked the security for the launch, Emmi.
Besides, my mom wants me home right after school.

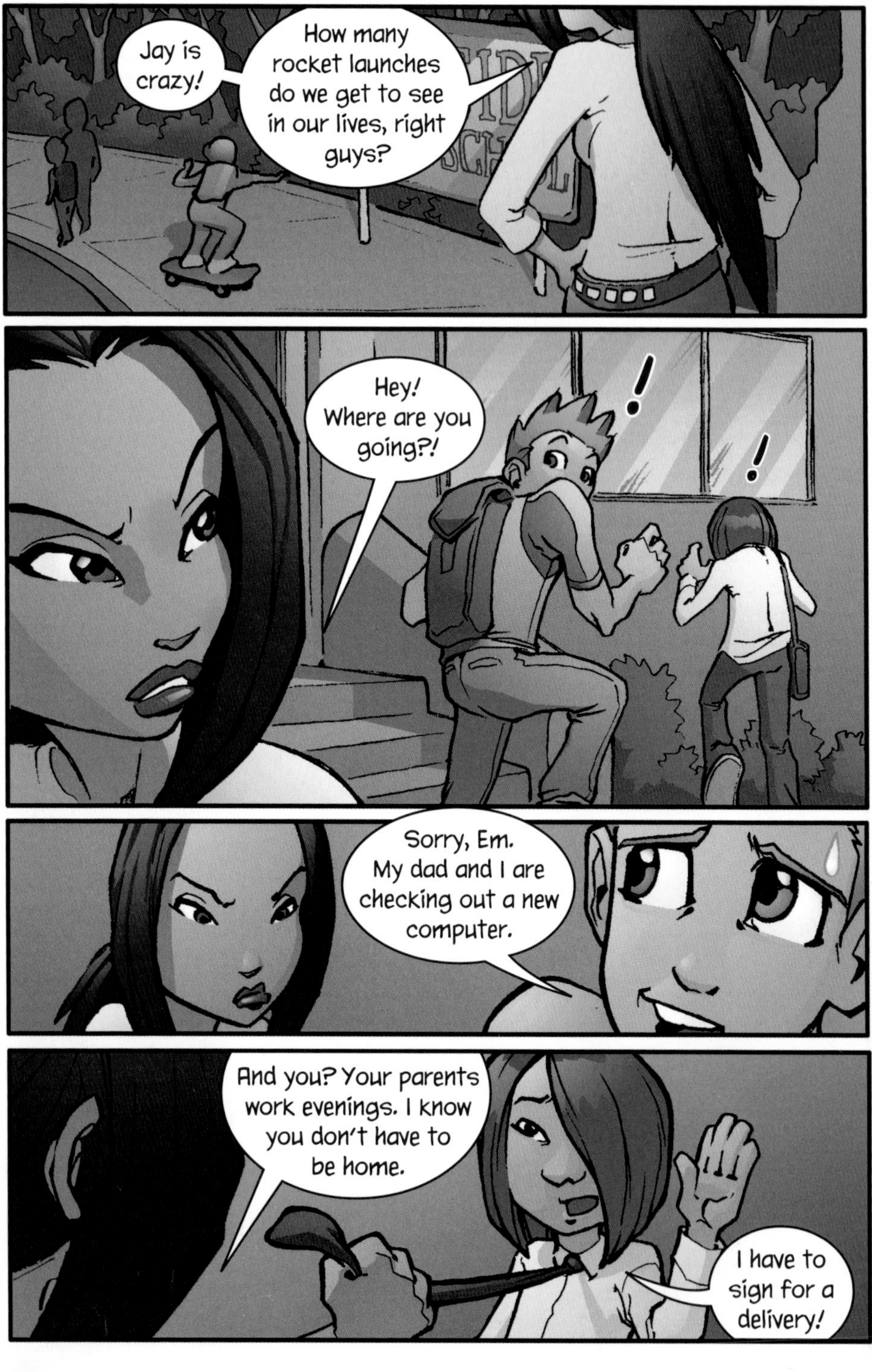
Jay is crazy!
How many rocket launches do we get to see in our lives, right guys?
!
!
Hey! Where are you going?!
Sorry, Em. My dad and I are checking out a new computer.
And you? Your parents work evenings. I know you don't have to be home.
I have to sign for a delivery!

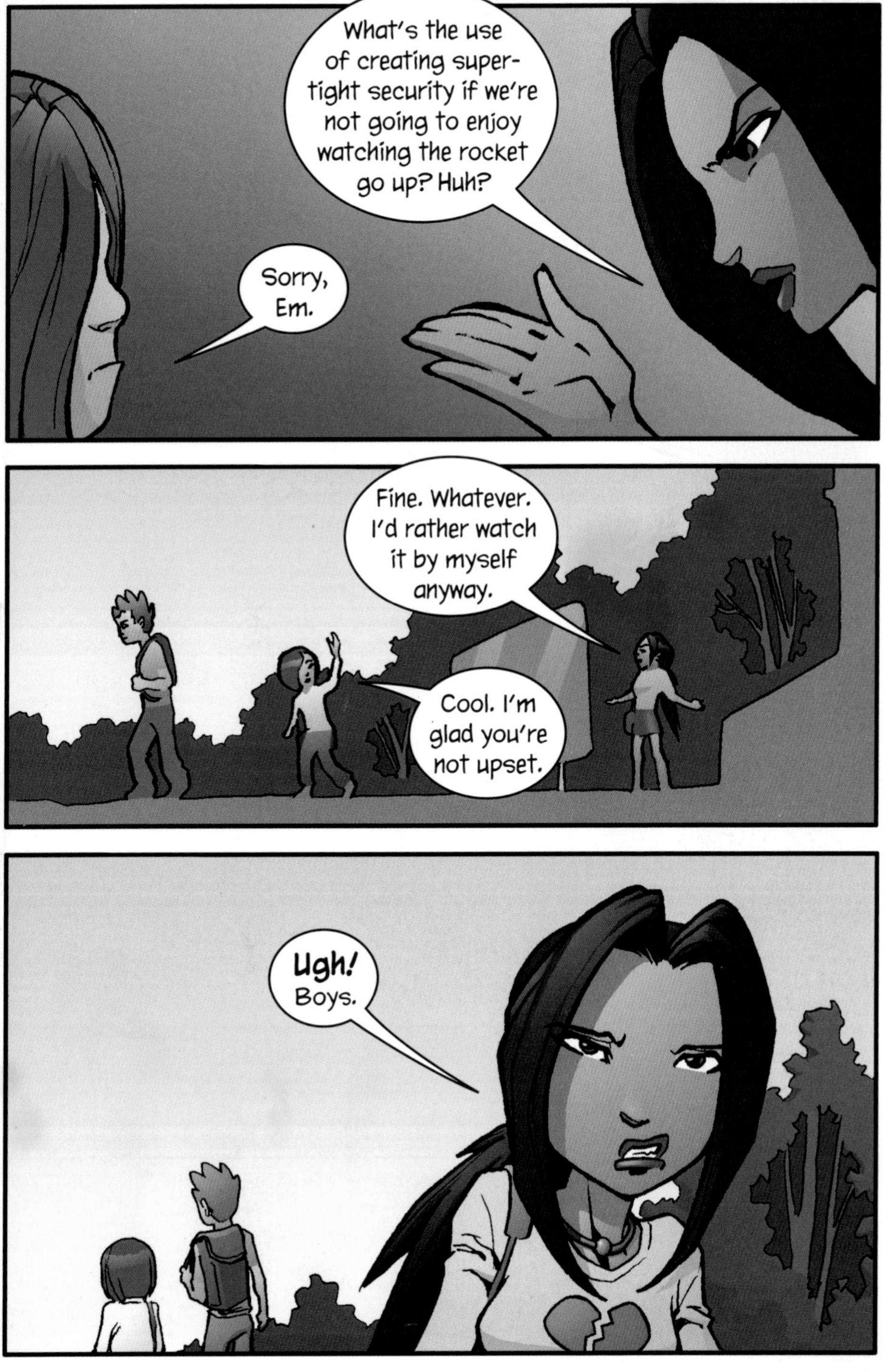
What's the use of creating super-tight security if we're not going to enjoy watching the rocket go up? Huh?
Sorry, Em.
Fine. Whatever. I'd rather watch it by myself anyway.
Cool. I'm glad you're not upset.
Ugh! Boys.

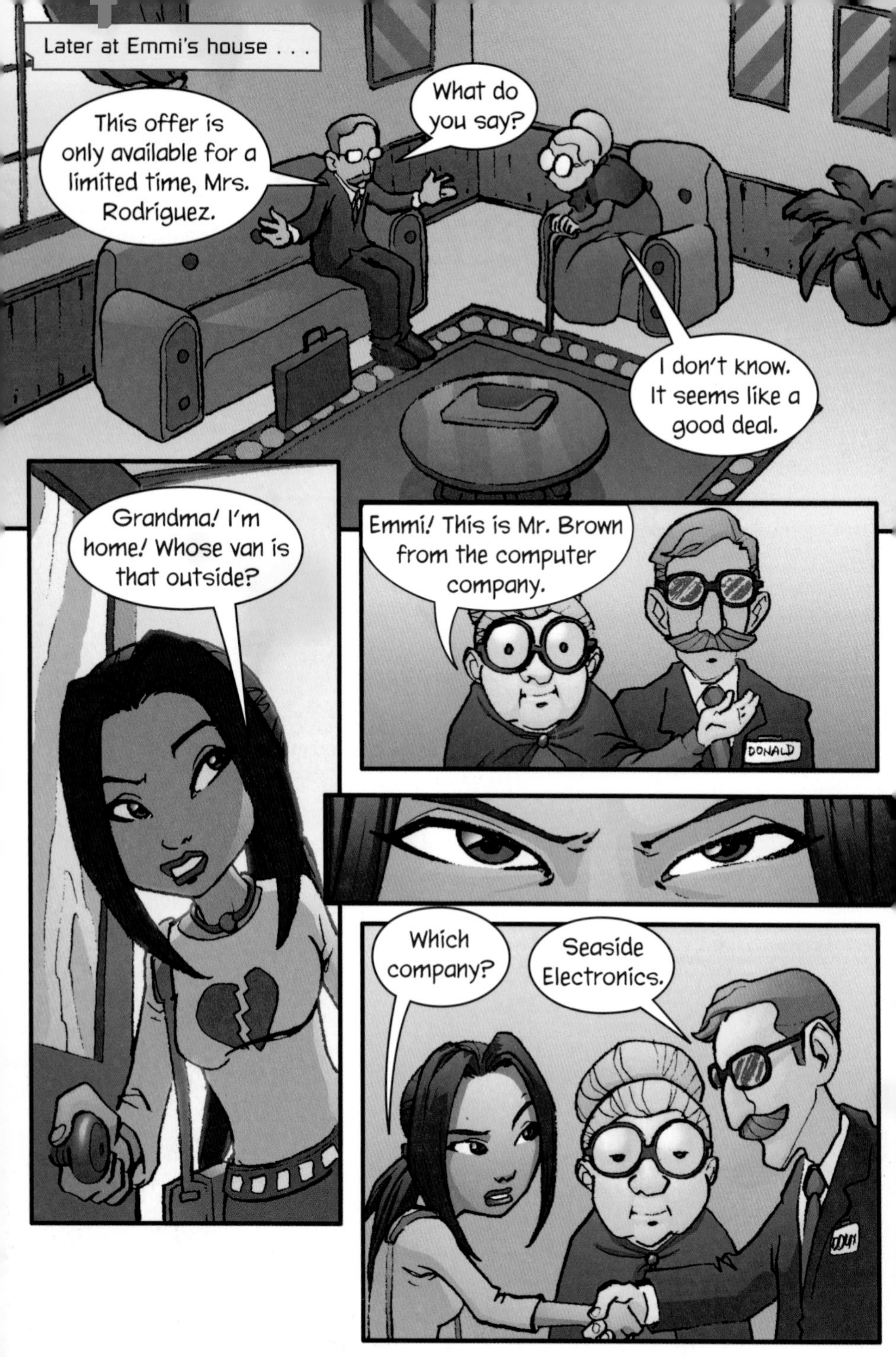
Later at Emmi's house . . .
This offer is only available for a limited time, Mrs. Rodriguez.
What do you say?
I don't know. It seems like a good deal.
Grandma! I'm home! Whose van is that outside?
Emmi! This is Mr. Brown from the computer company.
DONALD
Which company?
Seaside Electronics.

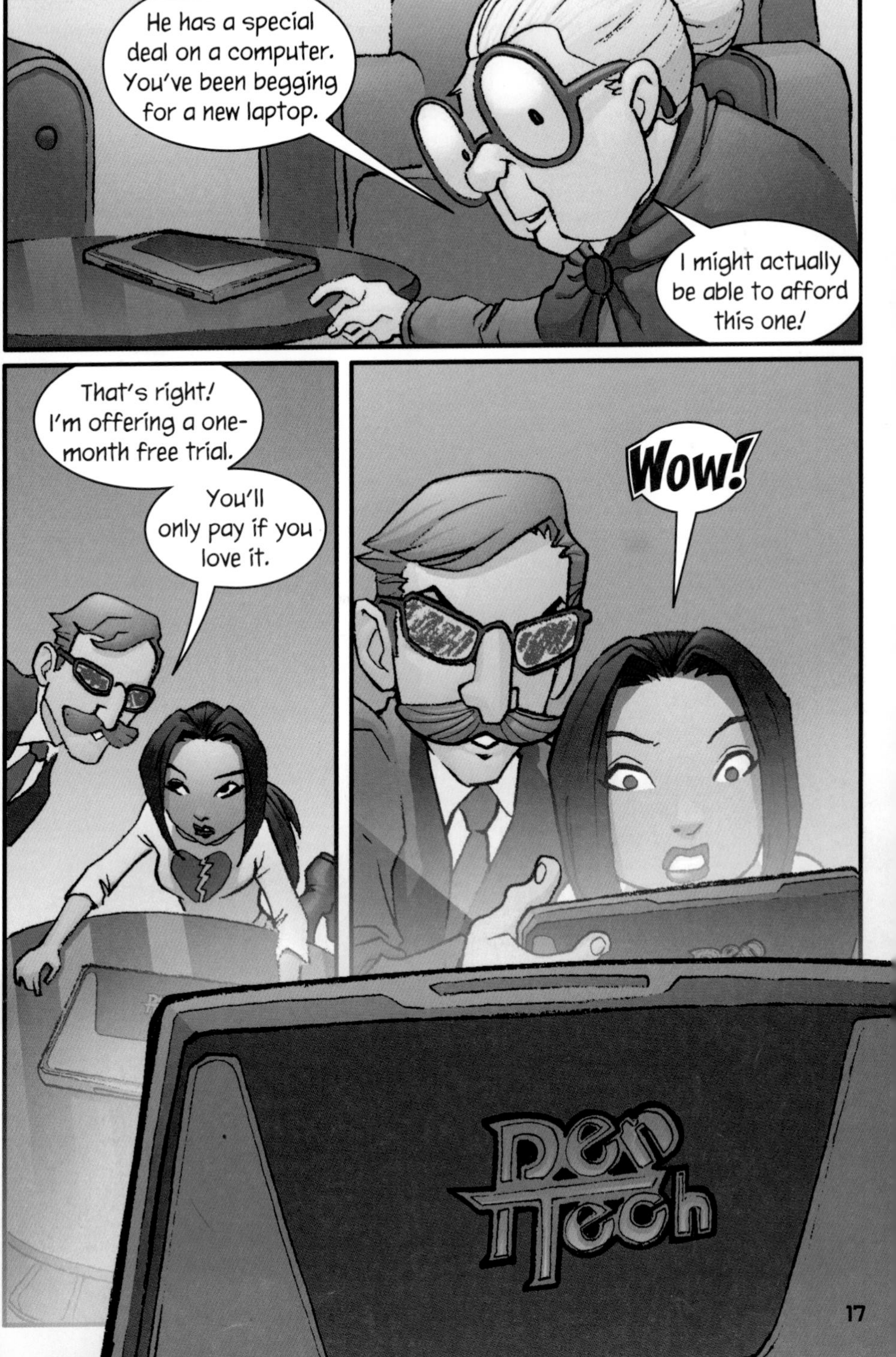
He has a special deal on a computer. You've been begging for a new laptop.
I might actually be able to afford this one!
That's right! I'm offering a one-month free trial.
You'll only pay if you love it.
Wow!
Pen Tech

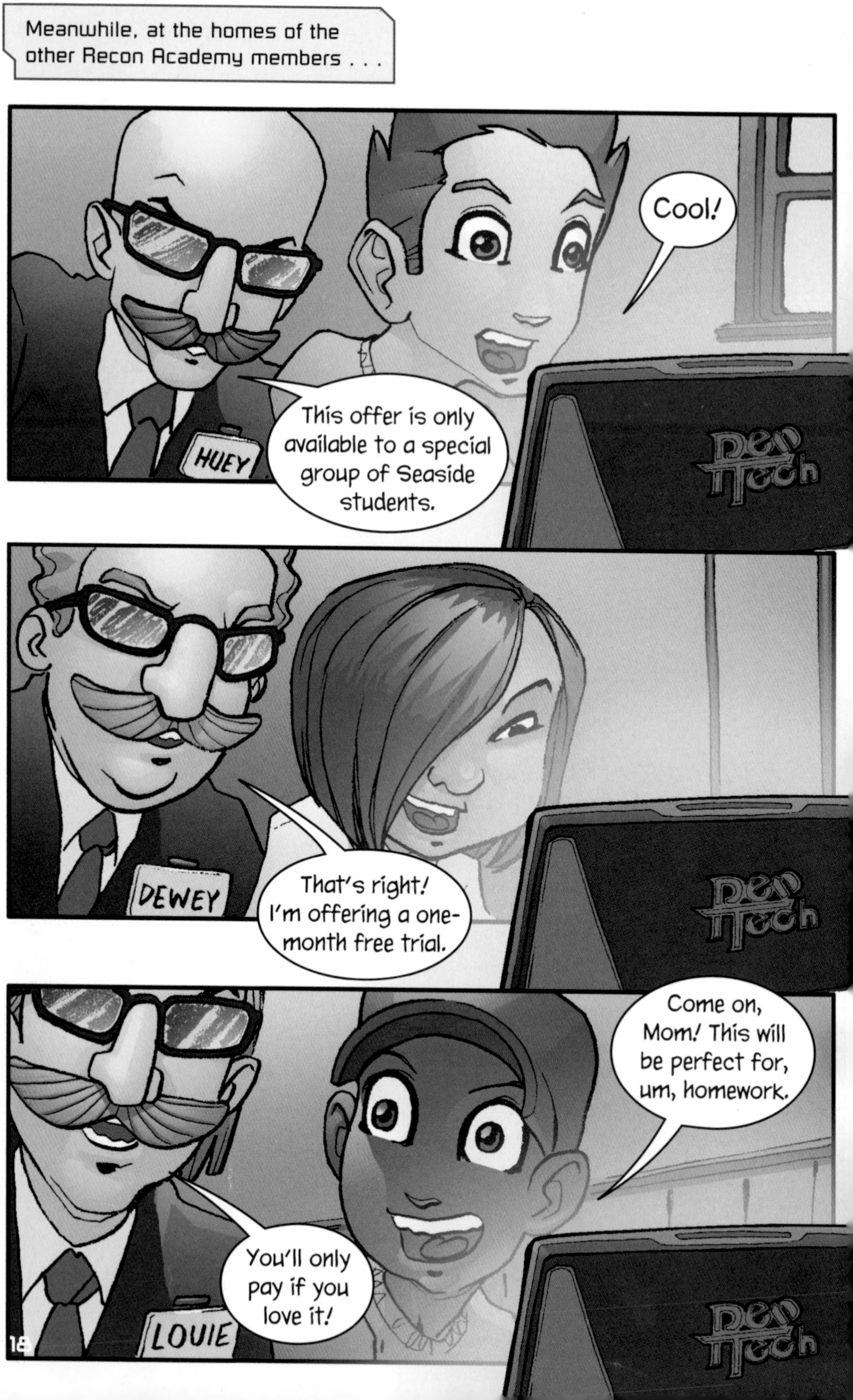
Meanwhile, at the homes of the other Recon Academy members . . .
Cool!
This offer is only available to a special group of Seaside students.
HUEY
DesTech
That's right! I'm offering a one-month free trial.
DEWEY
DesTech
Come on, Mom! This will be perfect for, um, homework.
You'll only pay if you love it!
LOUIE
DesTech

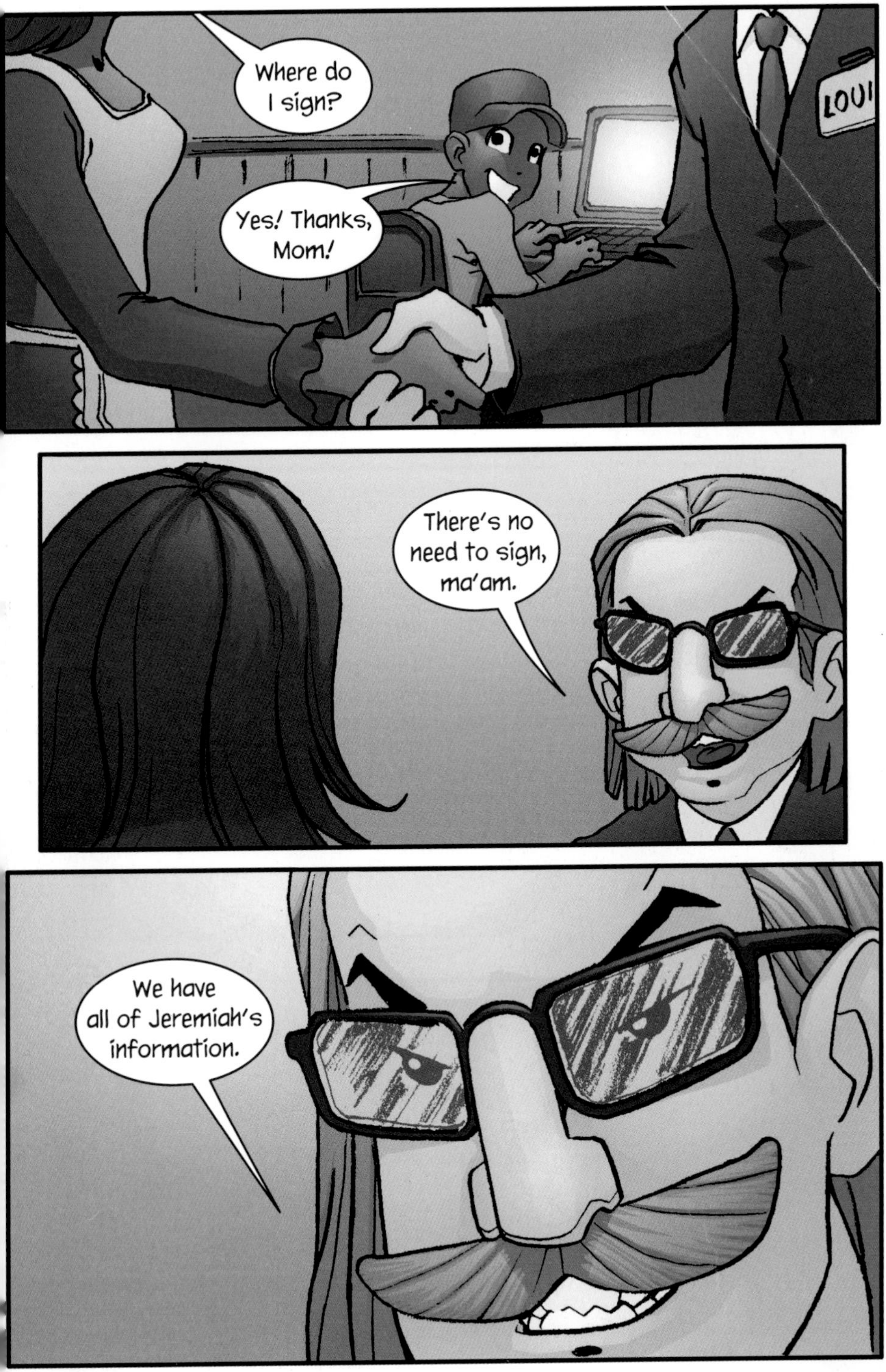
Where do I sign?
Yes! Thanks, Mom!
LOUI
There's no need to sign, ma'am.
We have all of Jeremiah's information.

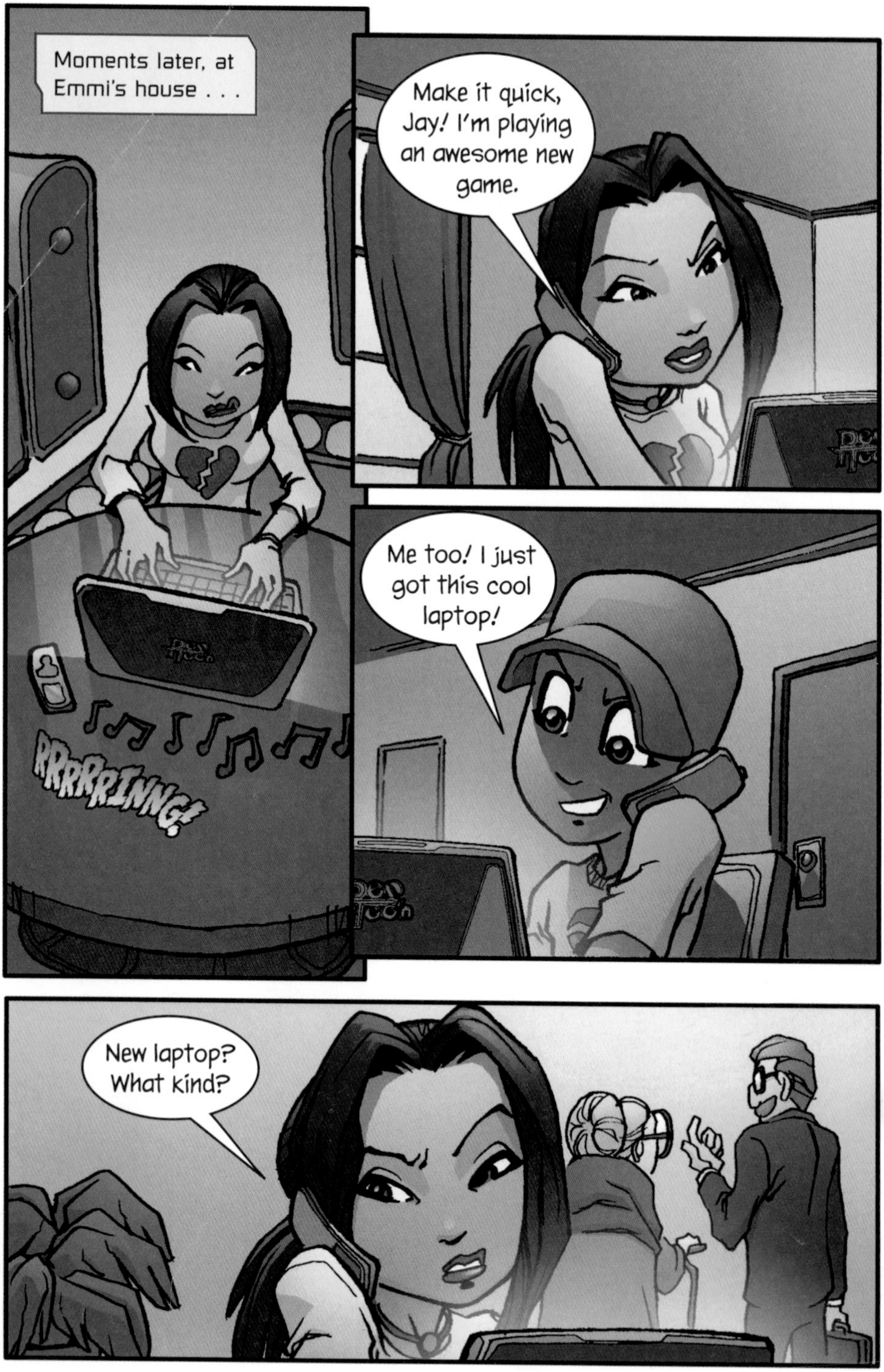
Moments later, at Emmi's house . . .
RRRRRINNG!
Make it quick, Jay! I'm playing an awesome new game.
Me too! I just got this cool laptop!
New laptop? What kind?

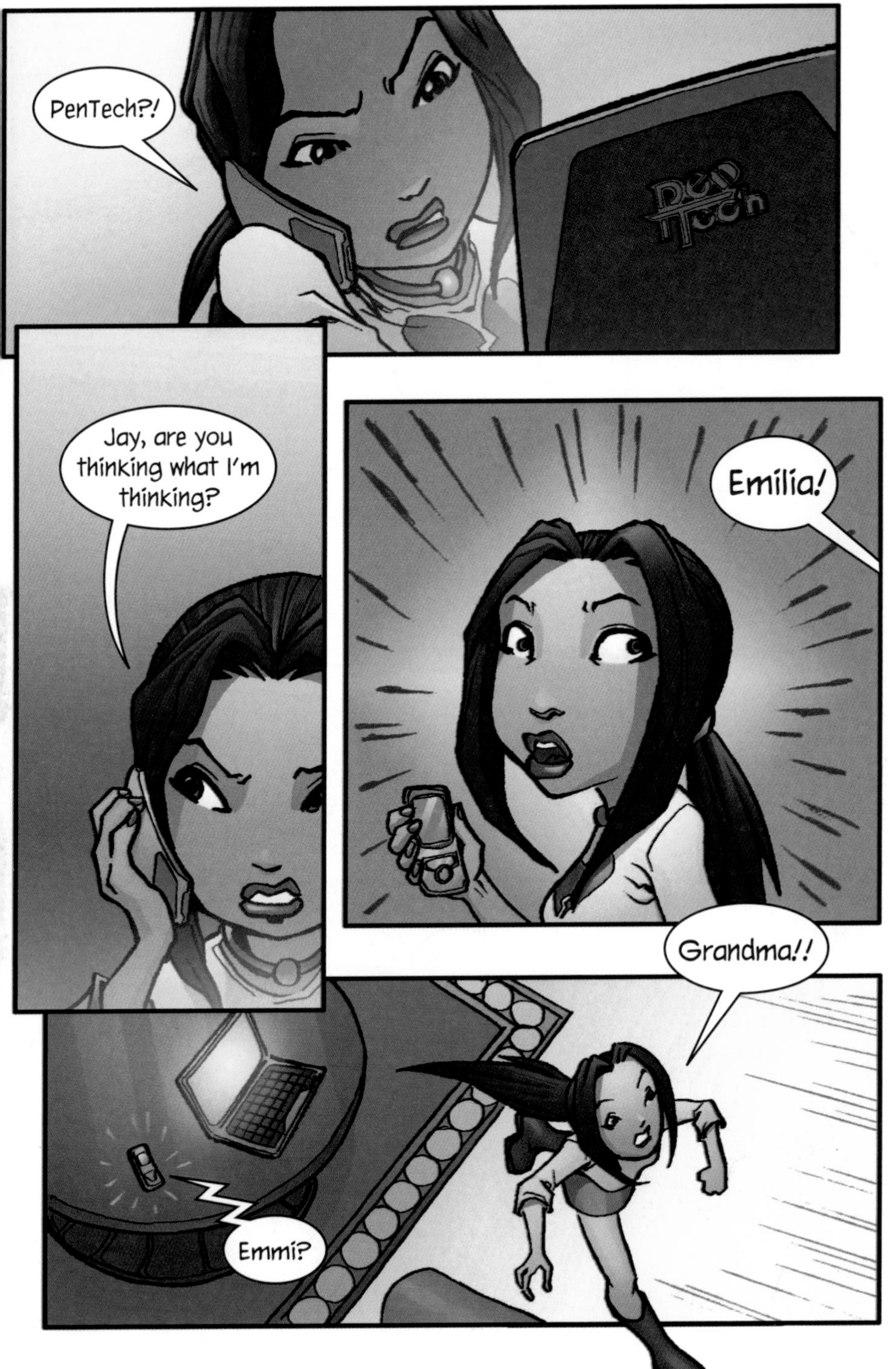
PenTech?!
Jay, are you thinking what I'm thinking?
Emilia!
Grandma!!
Emmi?

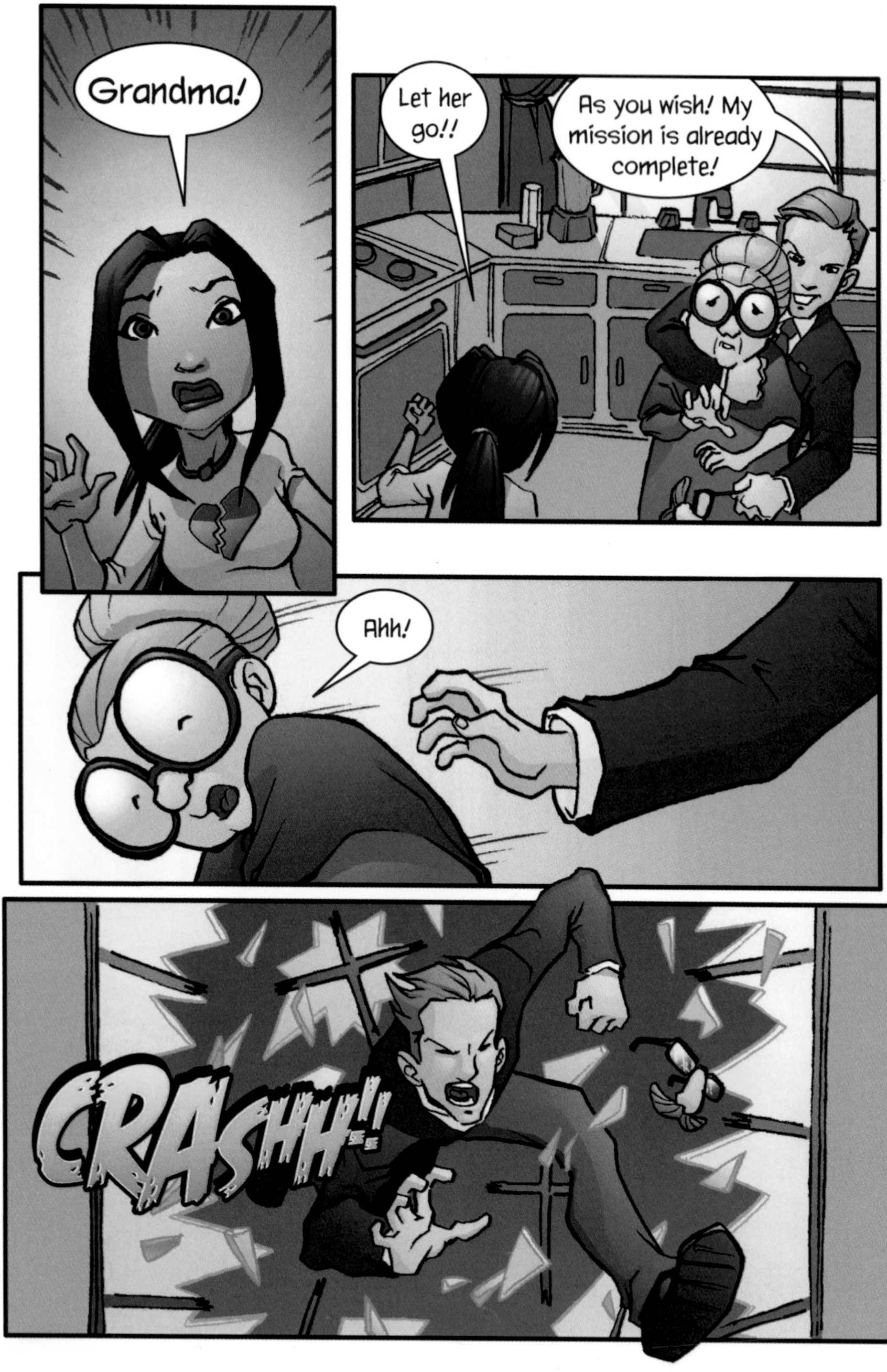
Grandma!
Let her go!!
As you wish! My mission is already complete!
Ahh!
CRASHH!!

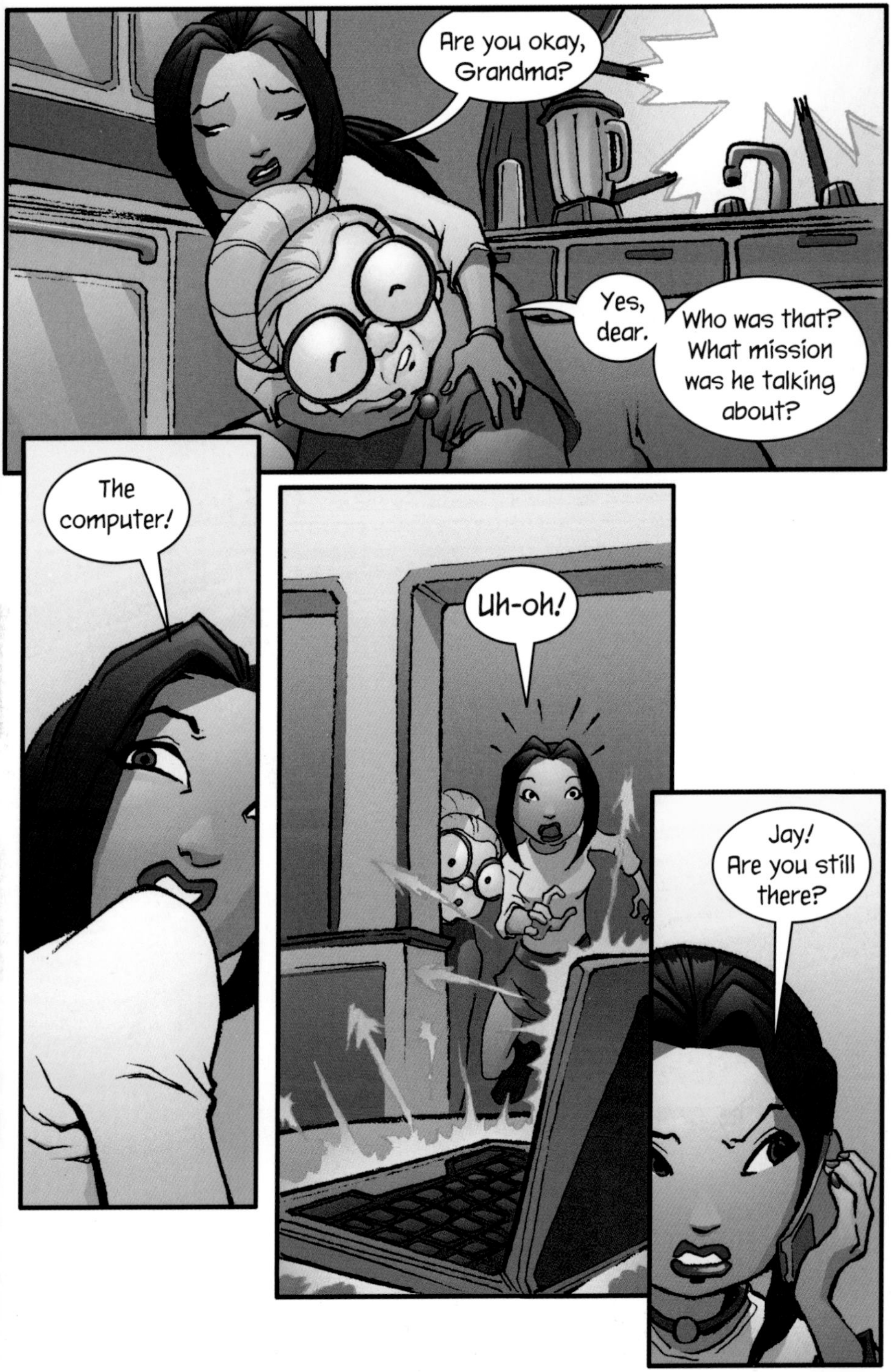
Are you okay, Grandma?
Yes, dear.
Who was that? What mission was he talking about?
The computer!
Uh-oh!
Jay! Are you still there?

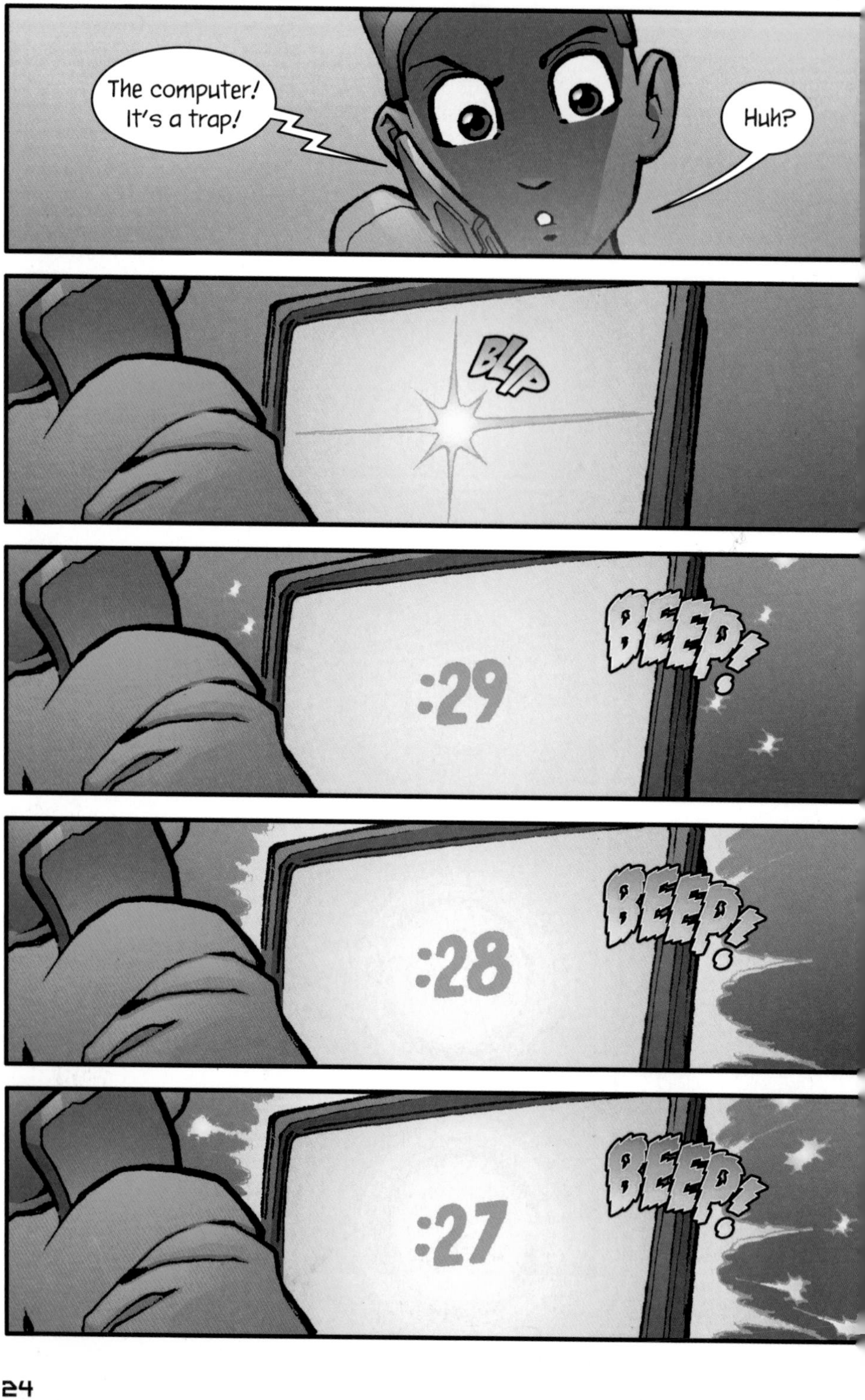
The computer! It's a trap!
Huh?
BLIP
:29
BEEP!
:28
BEEP!
:27
BEEP!

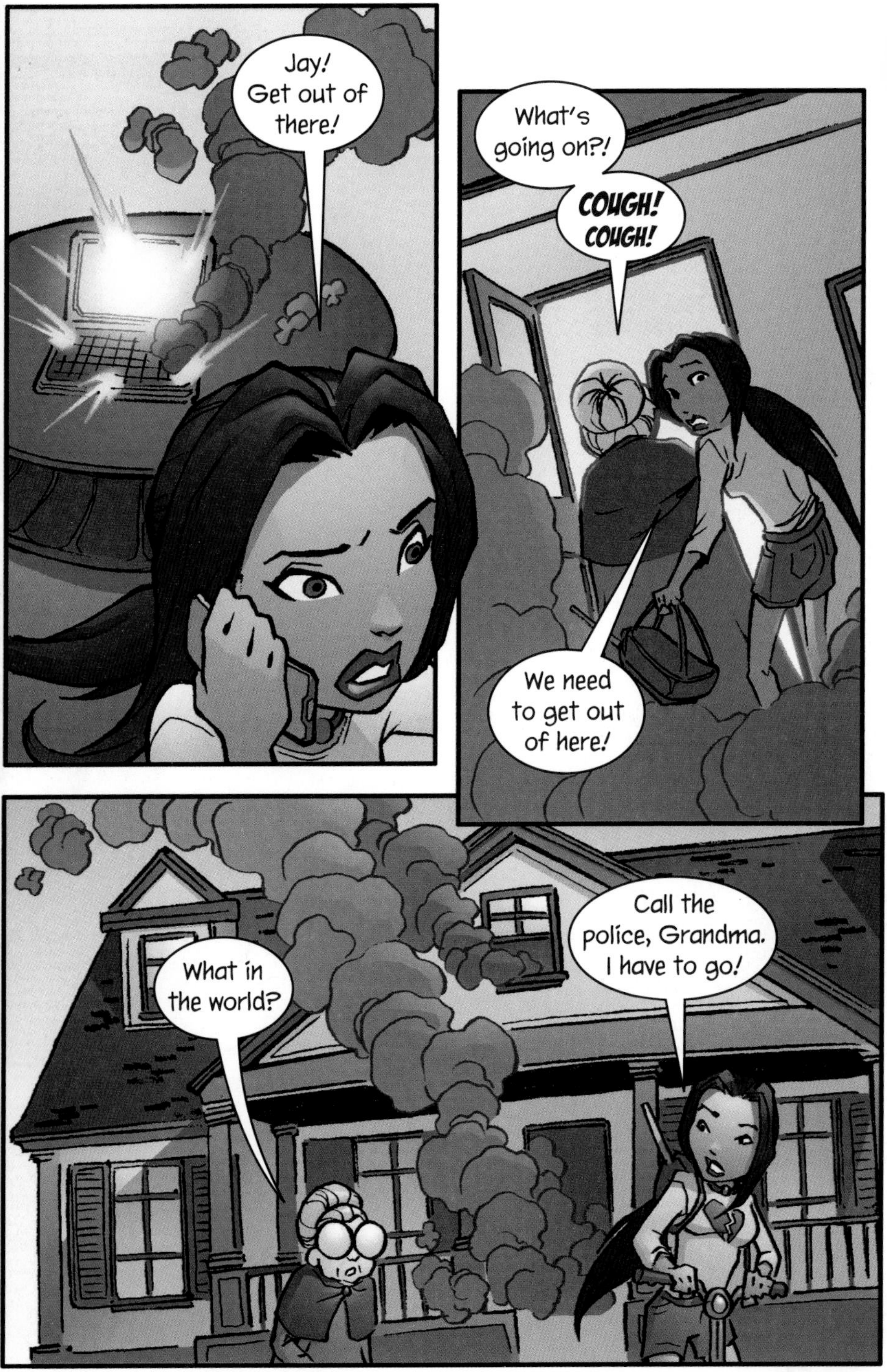
Jay! Get out of there!
What's going on?!
COUGH! COUGH!
We need to get out of here!
Call the police, Grandma. I have to go!
What in the world?

SECTION 3

FILE NO.
1437578

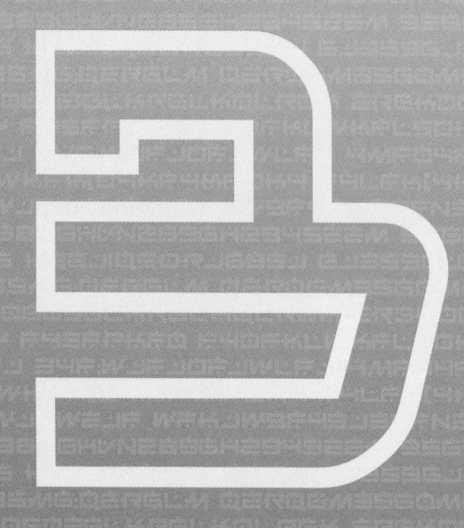

ACCESS GRANTED ››››

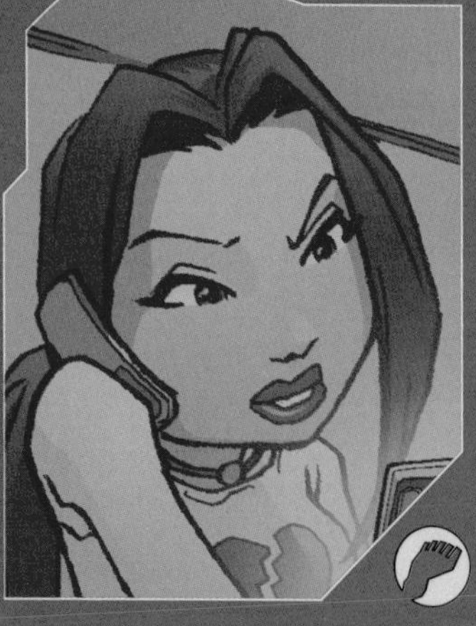

EMMI
MARTIAL ARTS

8579
1564574
109201
192091
1992
745979

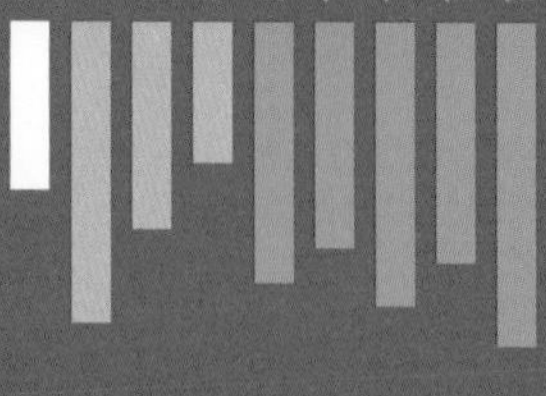

128718
293829
9283
98289
89
1
109201
192091
1992

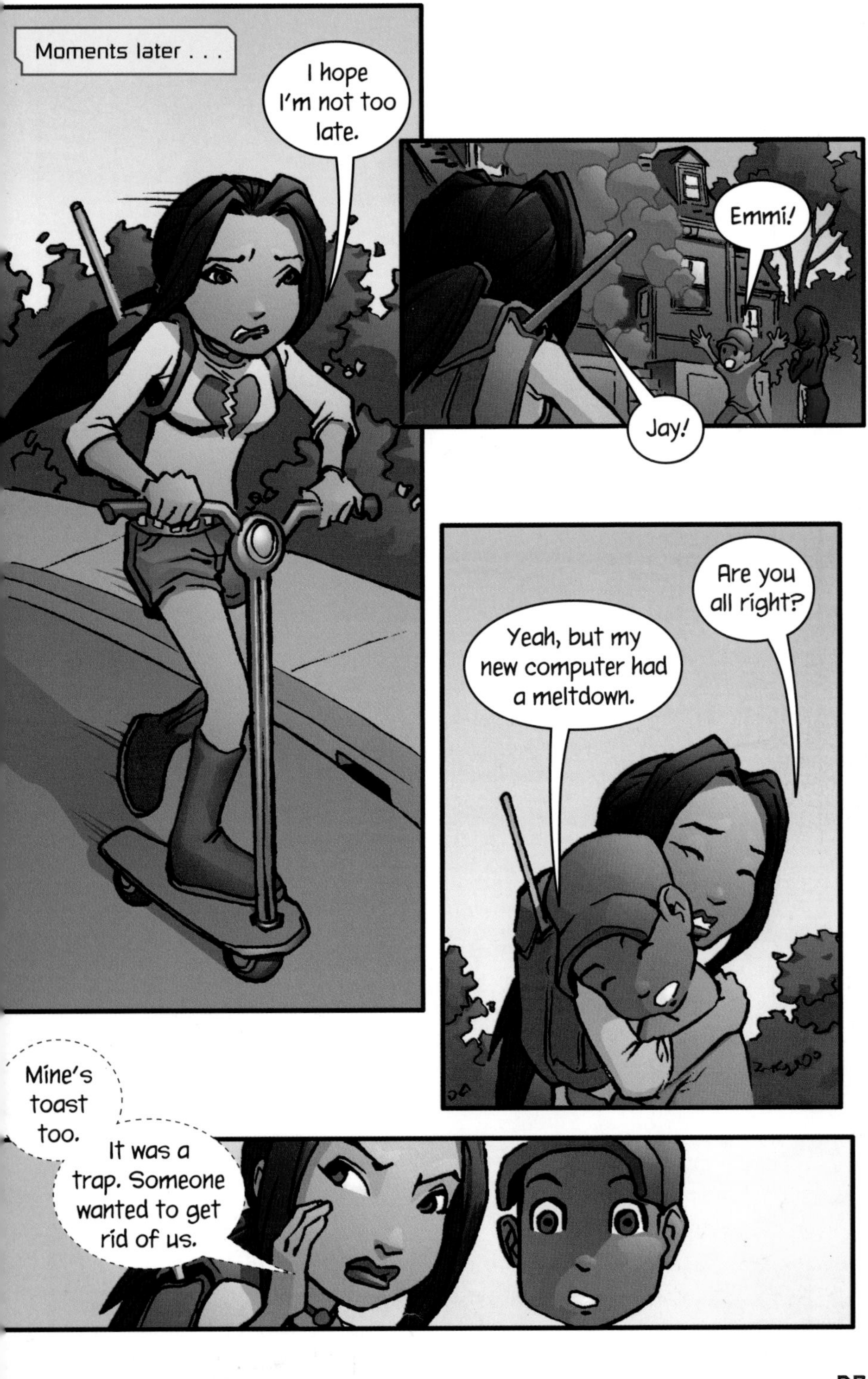
Moments later . . .
I hope I'm not too late.
Emmi!
Jay!
Are you all right?
Yeah, but my new computer had a meltdown.
Mine's toast too.
It was a trap. Someone wanted to get rid of us.

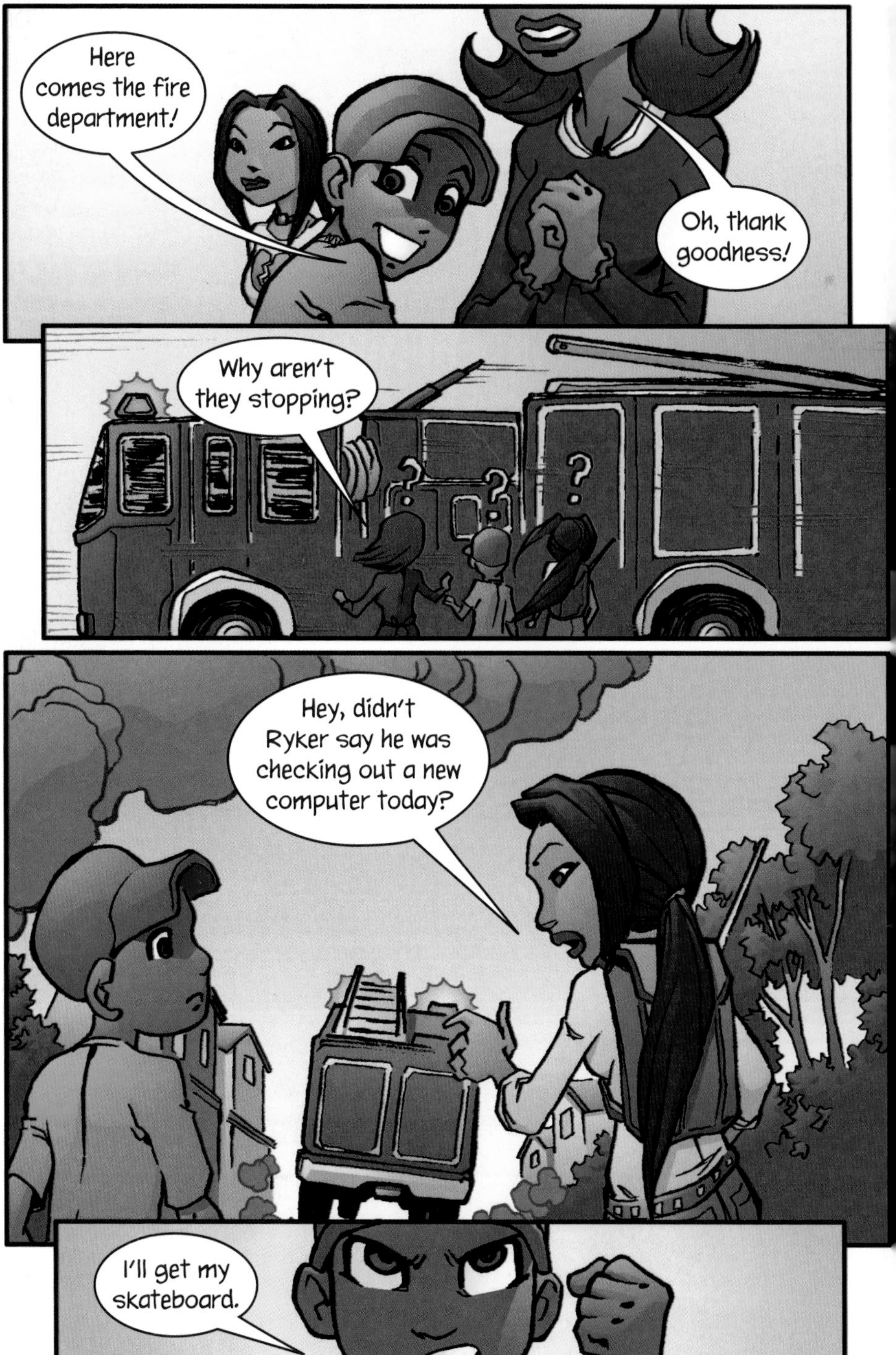
Here comes the fire department!
Oh, thank goodness!
Why aren't they stopping?
Hey, didn't Ryker say he was checking out a new computer today?
I'll get my skateboard.

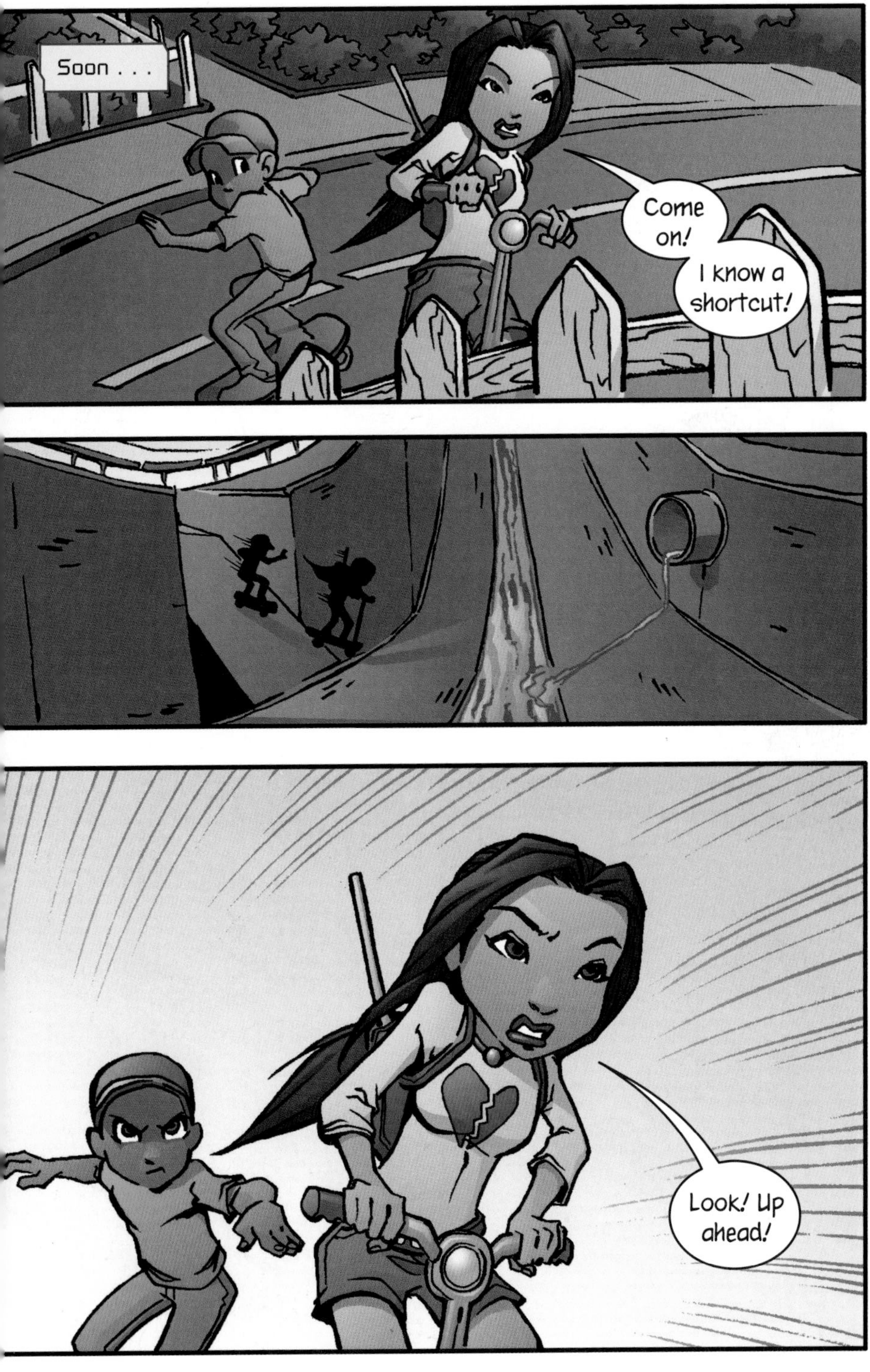
Soon . . .
Come on!
I know a shortcut!
Look! Up ahead!

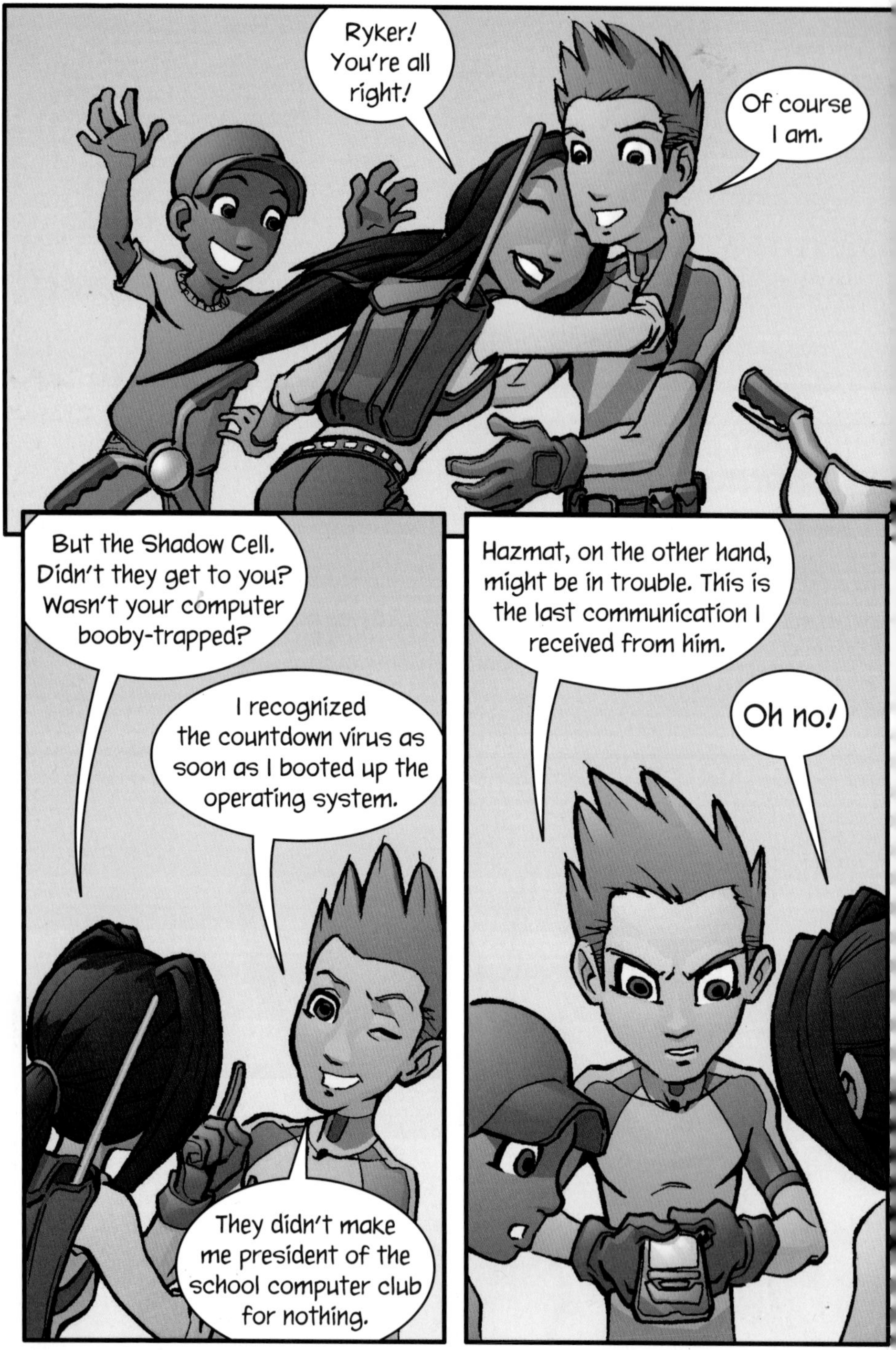
Ryker! You're all right!
Of course I am.
But the Shadow Cell. Didn't they get to you? Wasn't your computer booby-trapped?
I recognized the countdown virus as soon as I booted up the operating system.
They didn't make me president of the school computer club for nothing.
Hazmat, on the other hand, might be in trouble. This is the last communication I received from him.
Oh no!

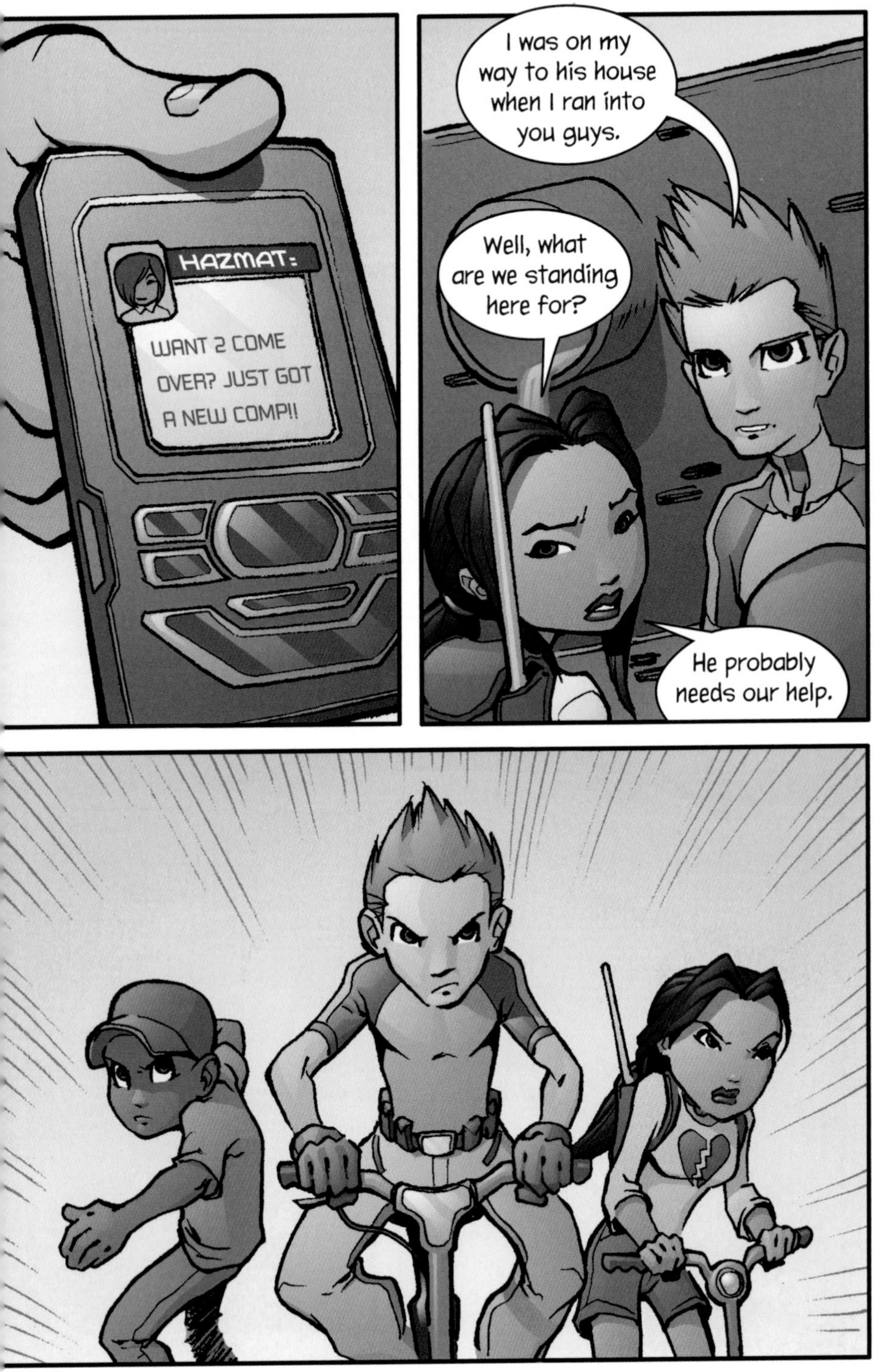
HAZMAT:
WANT 2 COME OVER? JUST GOT A NEW COMP!!
I was on my way to his house when I ran into you guys.
Well, what are we standing here for?
He probably needs our help.

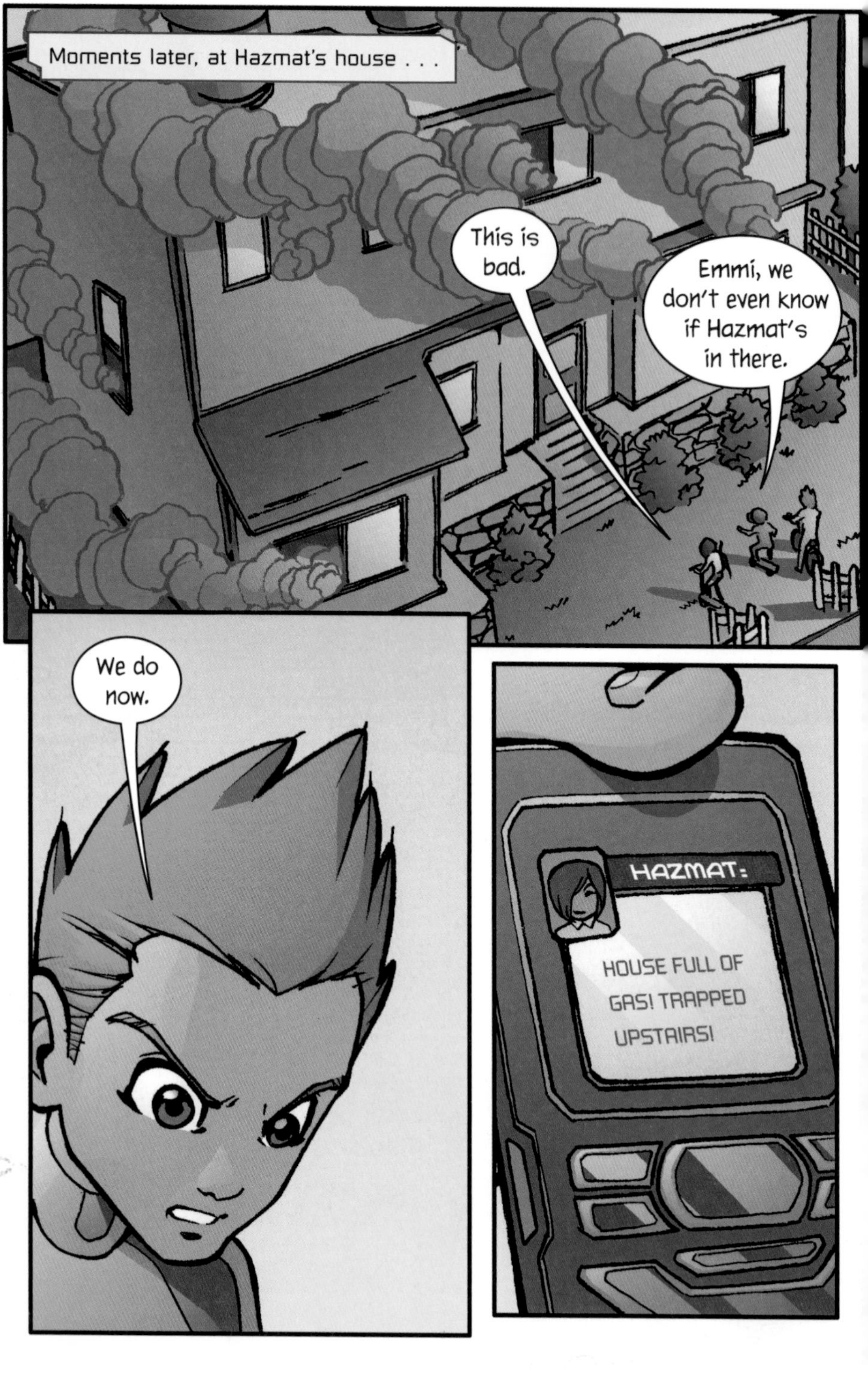
Moments later, at Hazmat's house . . .
This is bad.
Emmi, we don't even know if Hazmat's in there.
We do now.
HAZMAT:
HOUSE FULL OF GAS! TRAPPED UPSTAIRS!

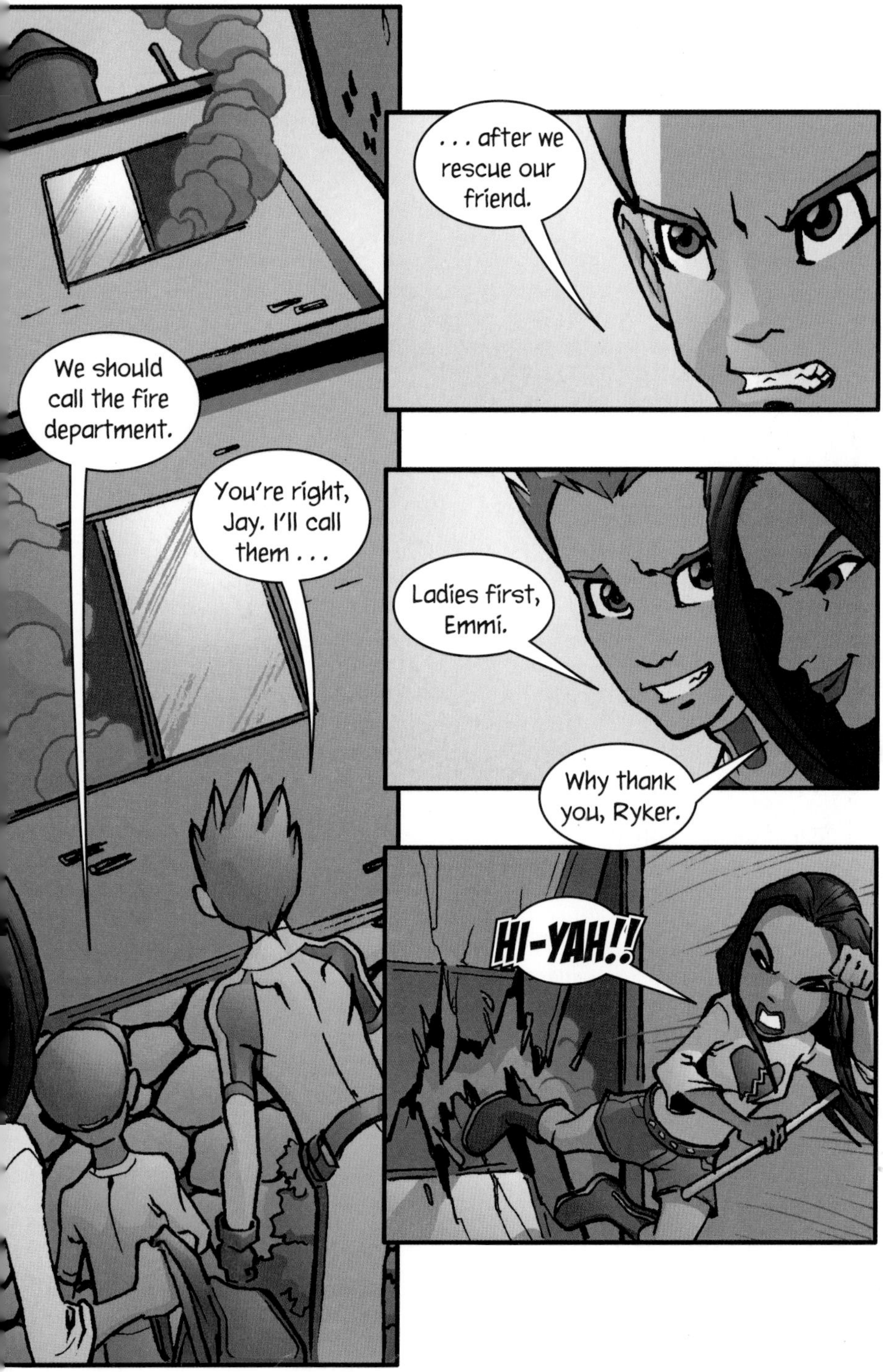

We should call the fire department.
You're right, Jay. I'll call them . . .
. . . after we rescue our friend.
Ladies first, Emmi.
Why thank you, Ryker.
HI-YAH!!

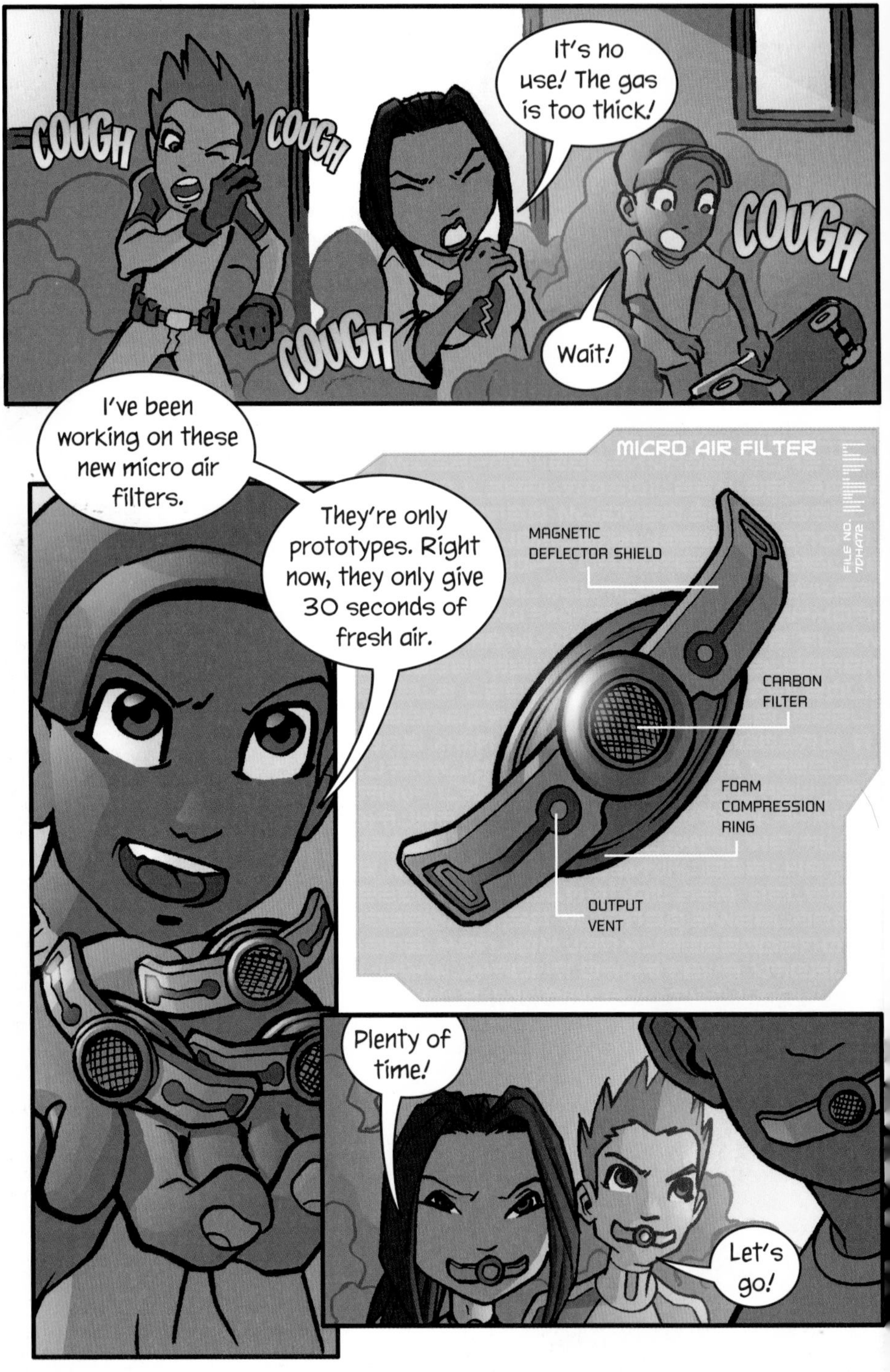
COUGH
COUGH
It's no use! The gas is too thick!
COUGH
COUGH
Wait!
I've been working on these new micro air filters.
They're only prototypes. Right now, they only give 30 seconds of fresh air.
MICRO AIR FILTER
FILE NO. 7DHA72
MAGNETIC DEFLECTOR SHIELD
CARBON FILTER
FOAM COMPRESSION RING
OUTPUT VENT
Plenty of time!
Let's go!

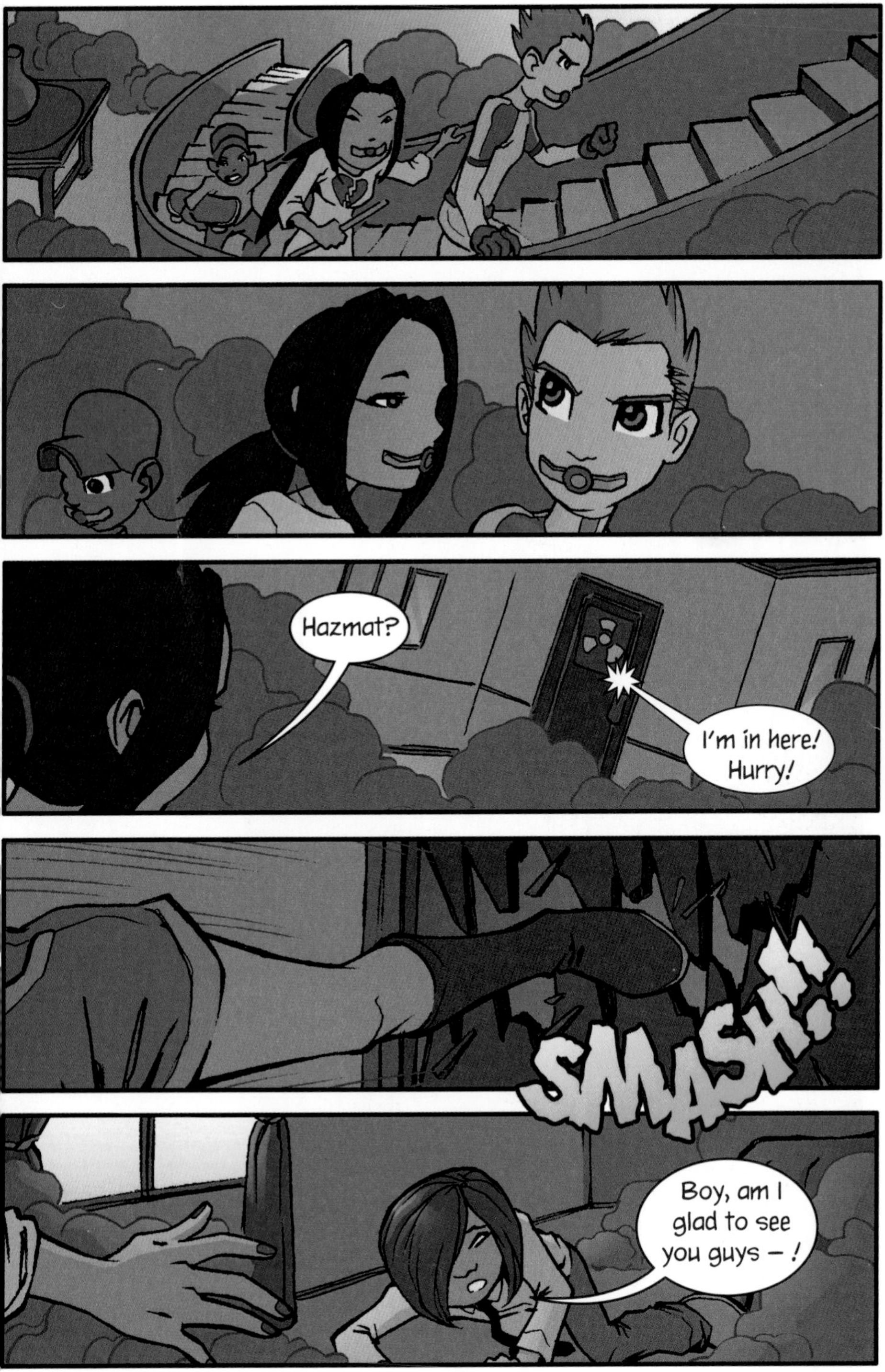
Hazmat?
I'm in here! Hurry!
SMASH!!!
Boy, am I glad to see you guys – !

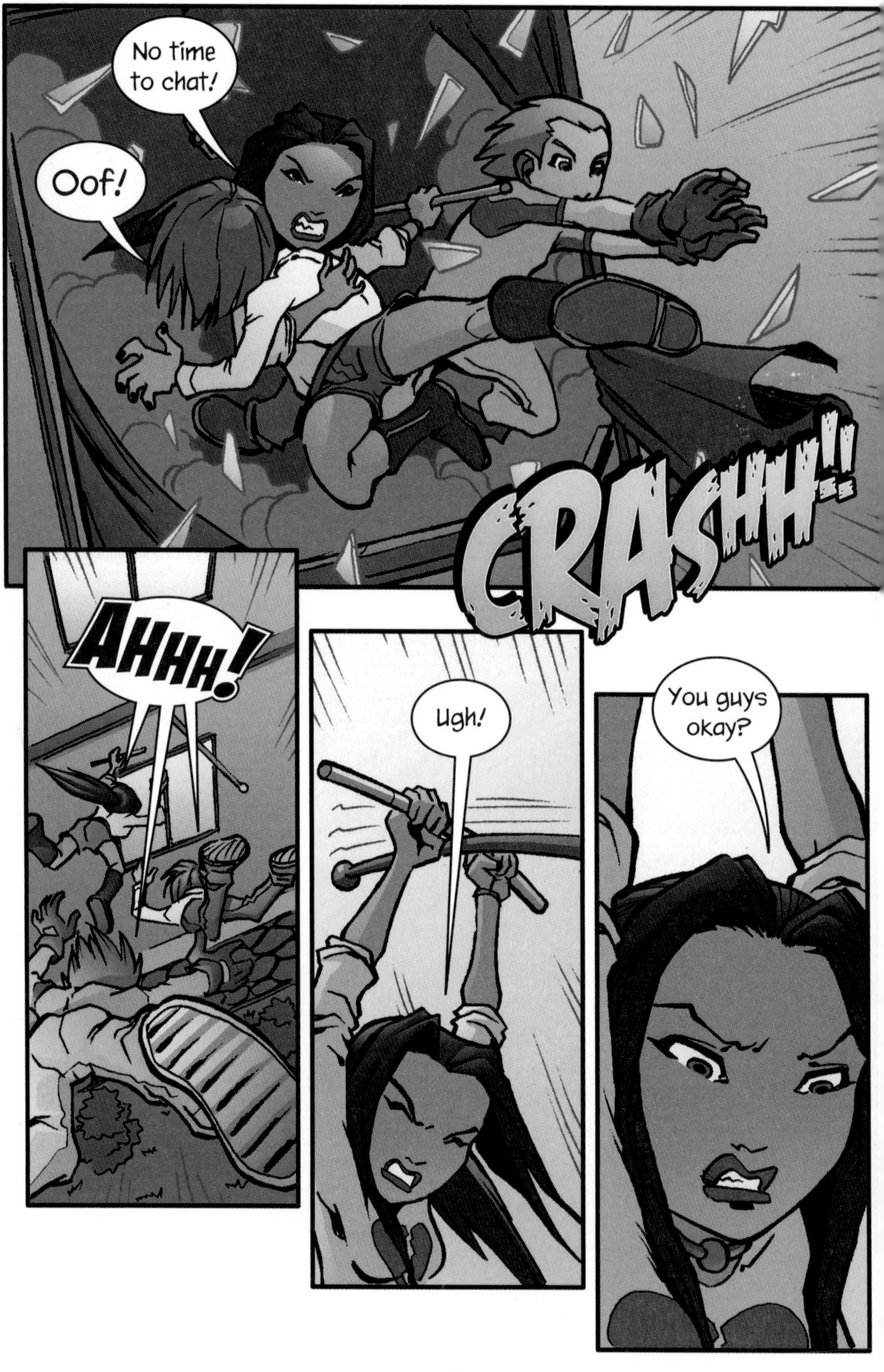
No time to chat!
Oof!
CRASHH!!
AHHH!
Ugh!
You guys okay?

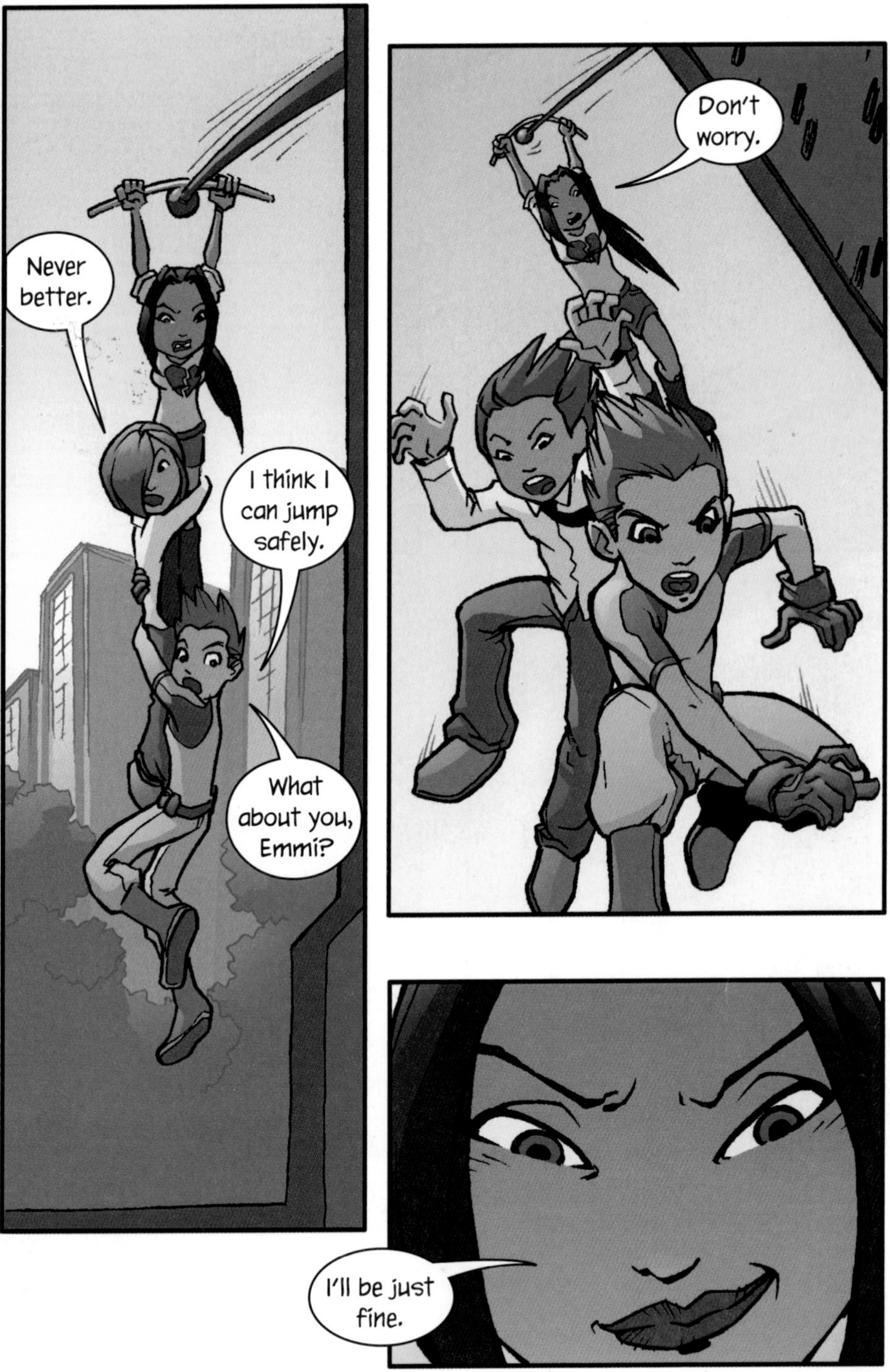
Never better.
I think I can jump safely.
What about you, Emmi?
Don't worry.
I'll be just fine.

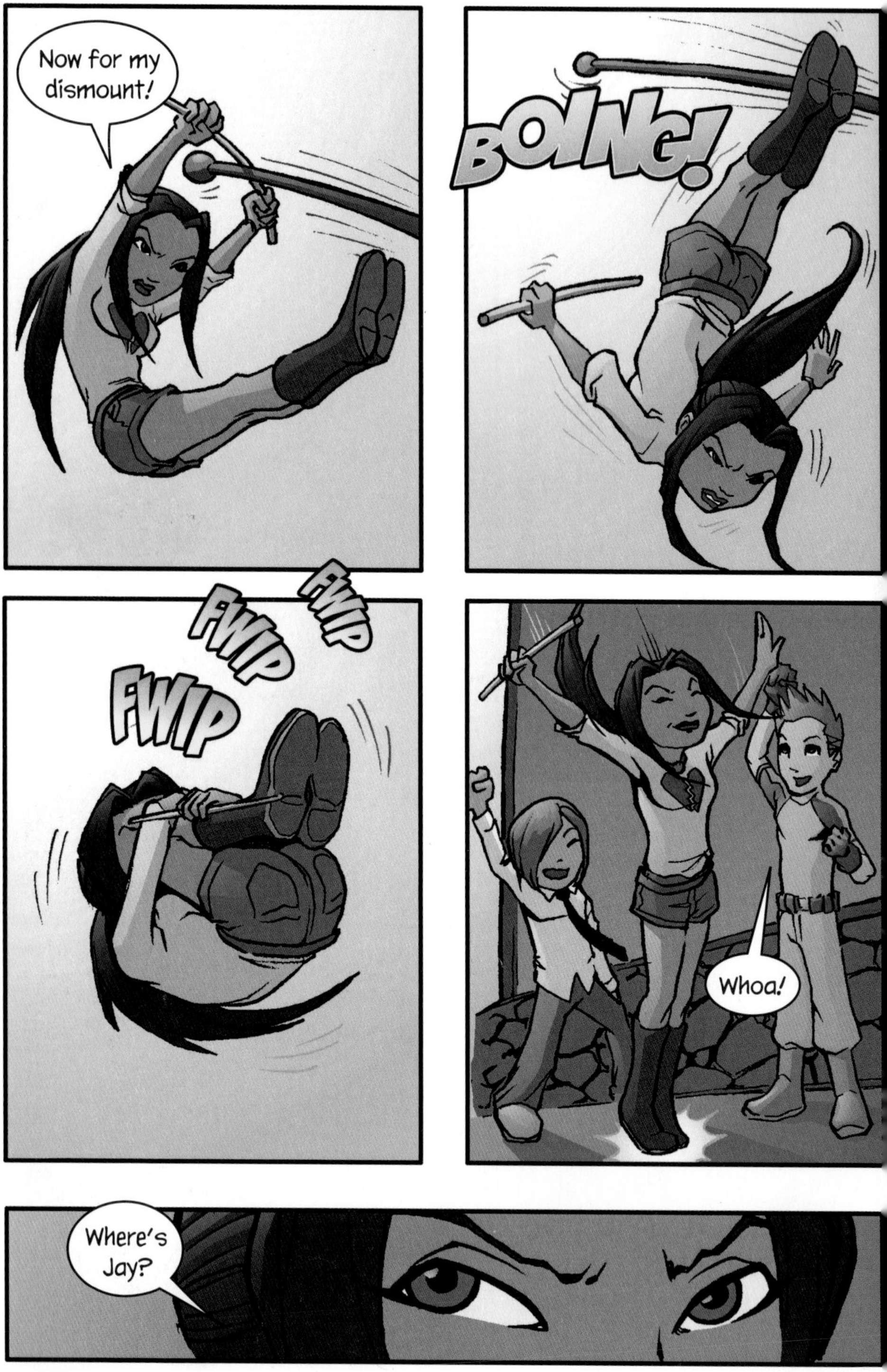
Now for my dismount!
BOING!
FWIP
FWIP
FWIP
Whoa!
Where's Jay?

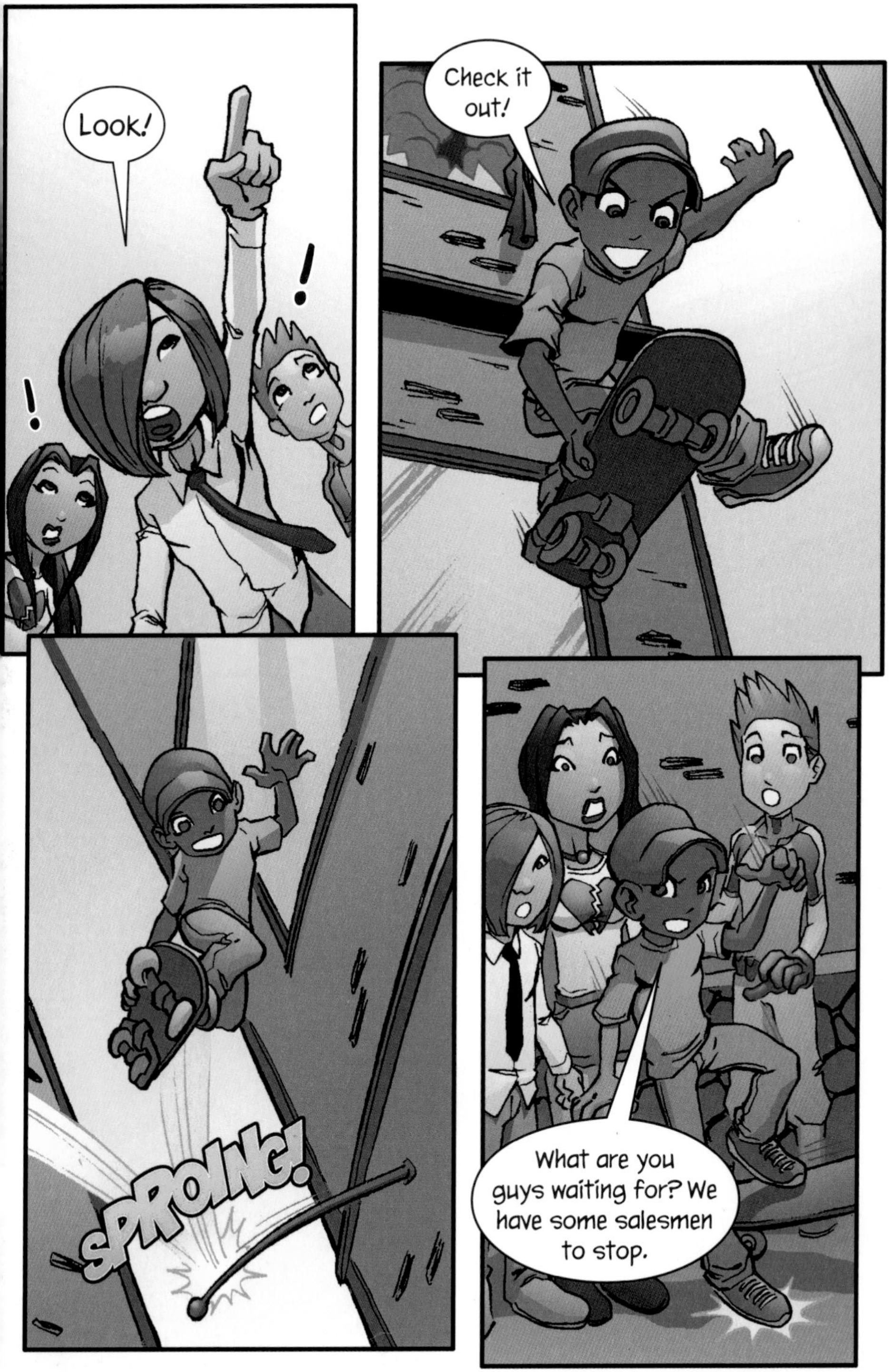
Look!
!
!
Check it out!
SPROING!
What are you guys waiting for? We have some salesmen to stop.

SECTION 4

FILE NO. 1437578

ACCESS GRANTED

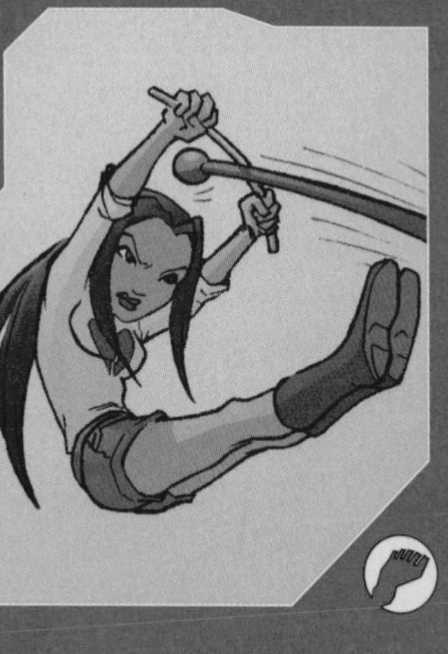

EMMI
MARTIAL ARTS

128718
293829
9283
98289
89
1
109201
192091
1992

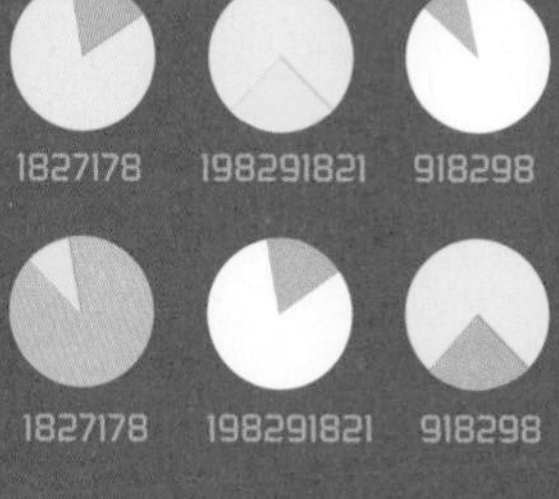
1827178
198291821
918298
1827178
198291821
918298

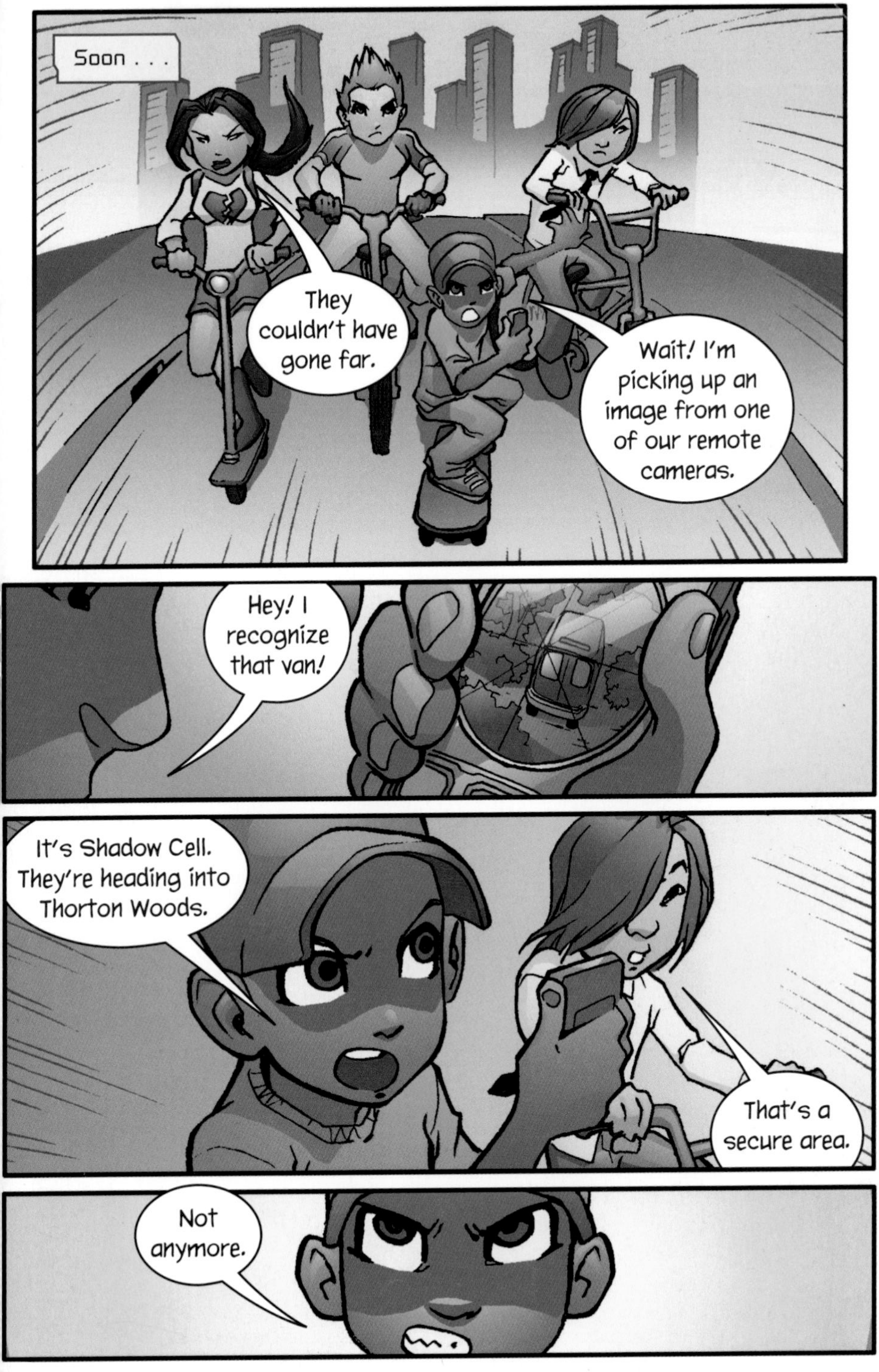
Soon . . .
They couldn't have gone far.
Wait! I'm picking up an image from one of our remote cameras.
Hey! I recognize that van!
It's Shadow Cell. They're heading into Thorton Woods.
That's a secure area.
Not anymore.

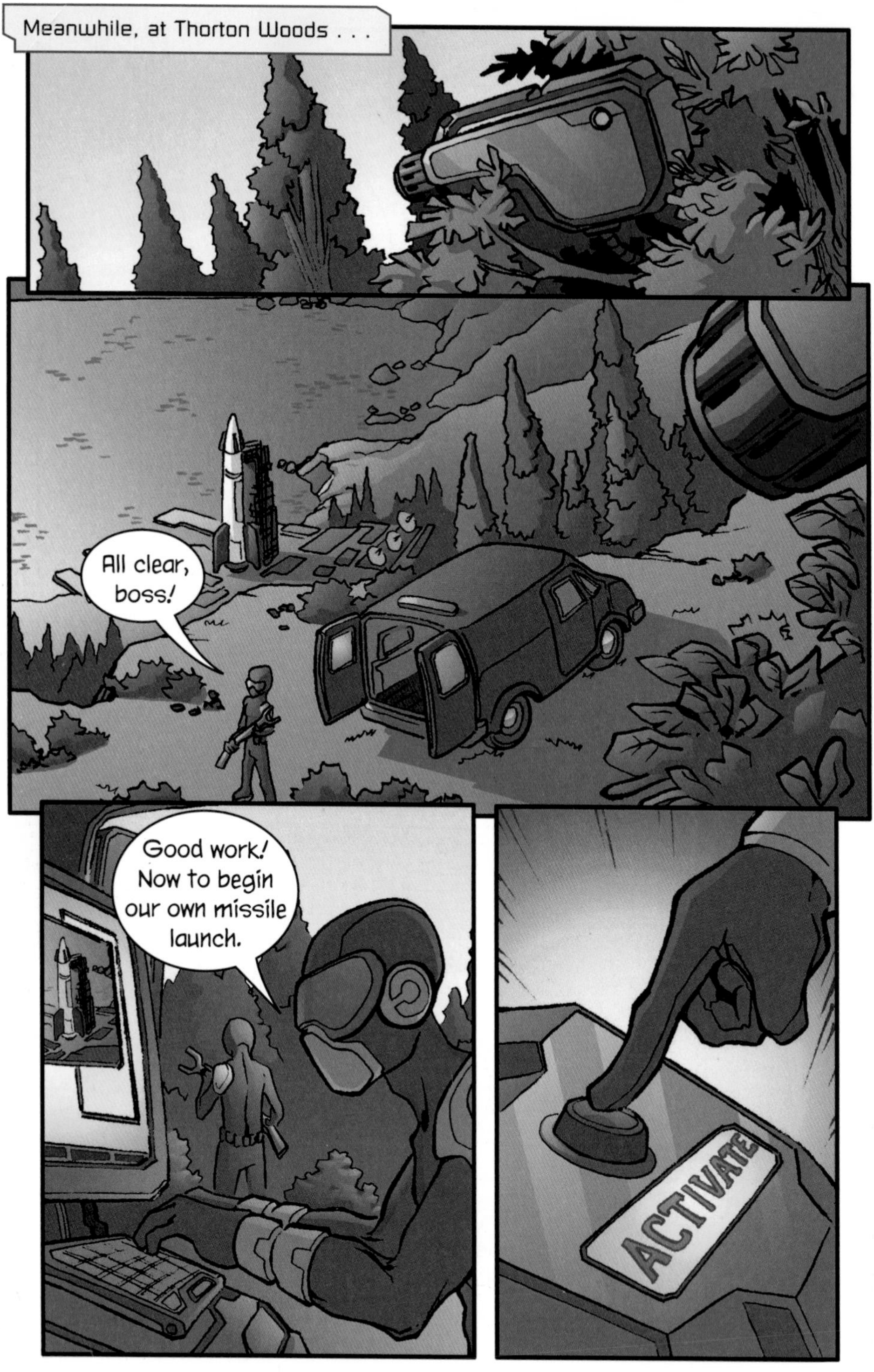
Meanwhile, at Thorton Woods . . .
All clear, boss!
Good work! Now to begin our own missile launch.
ACTIVATE

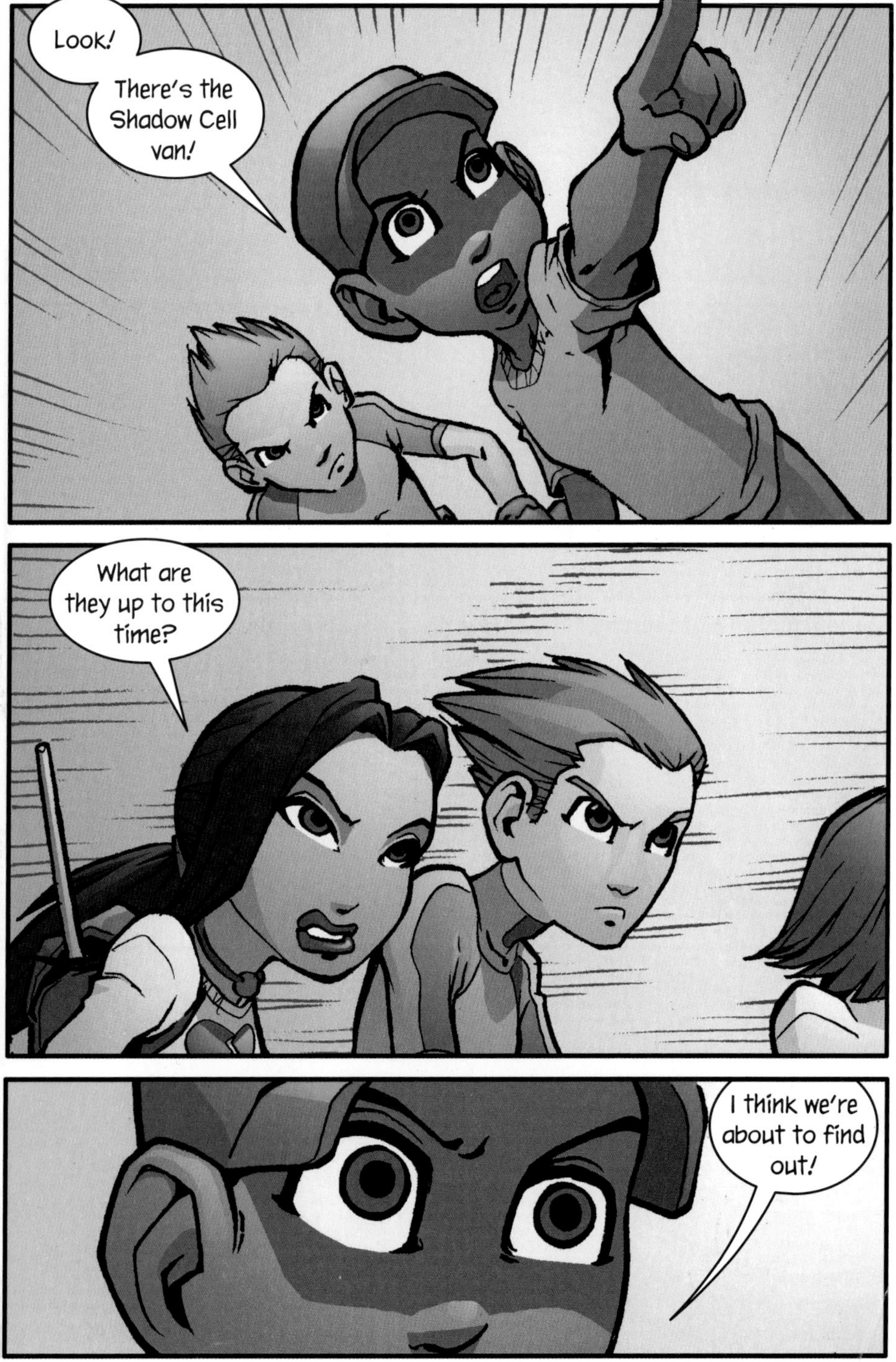
Look!
There's the Shadow Cell van!
What are they up to this time?
I think we're about to find out!

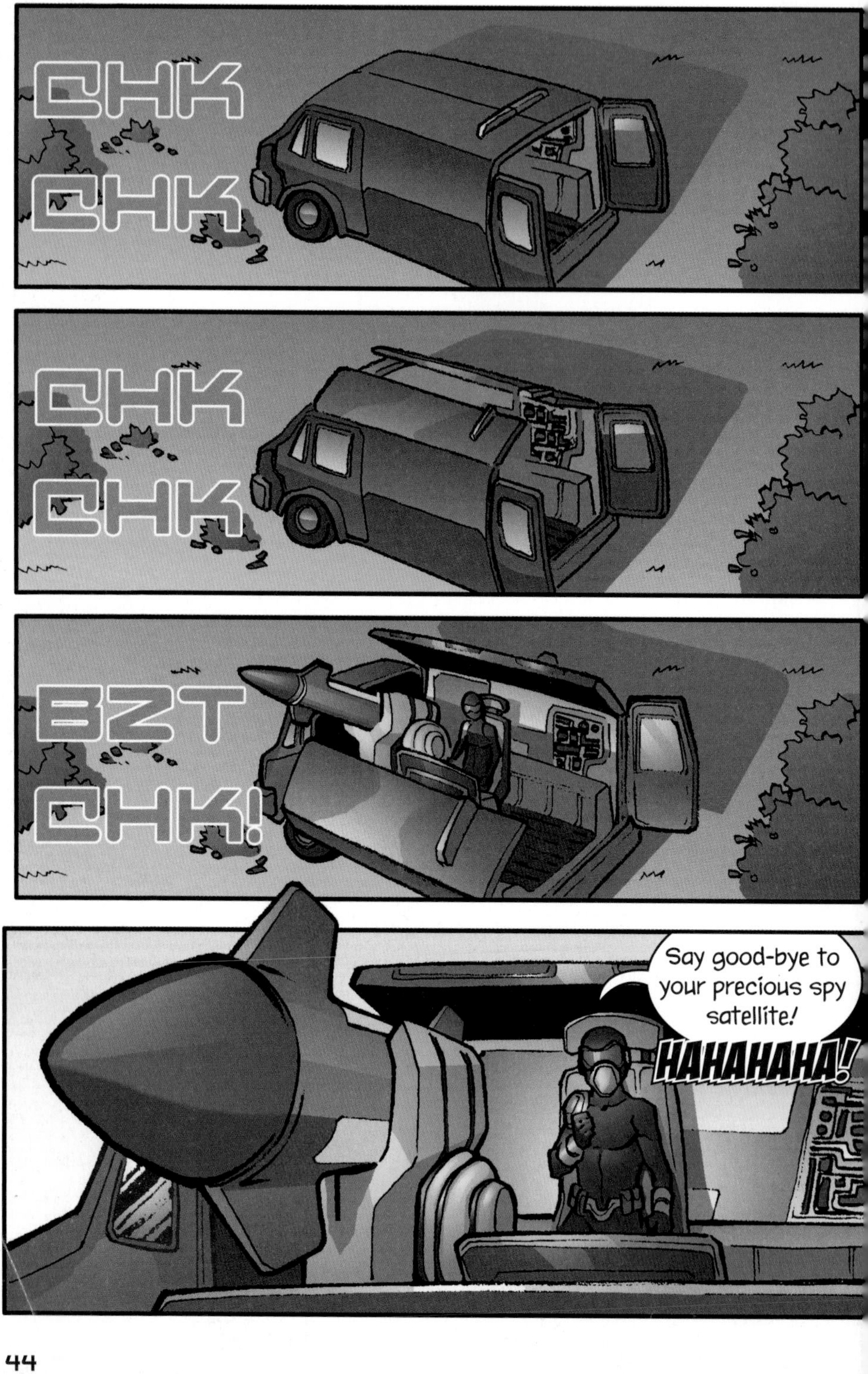
CHK
CHK
CHK
CHK
BZT
CHK!
Say good-bye to your precious spy satellite!
HAHAHAHA!

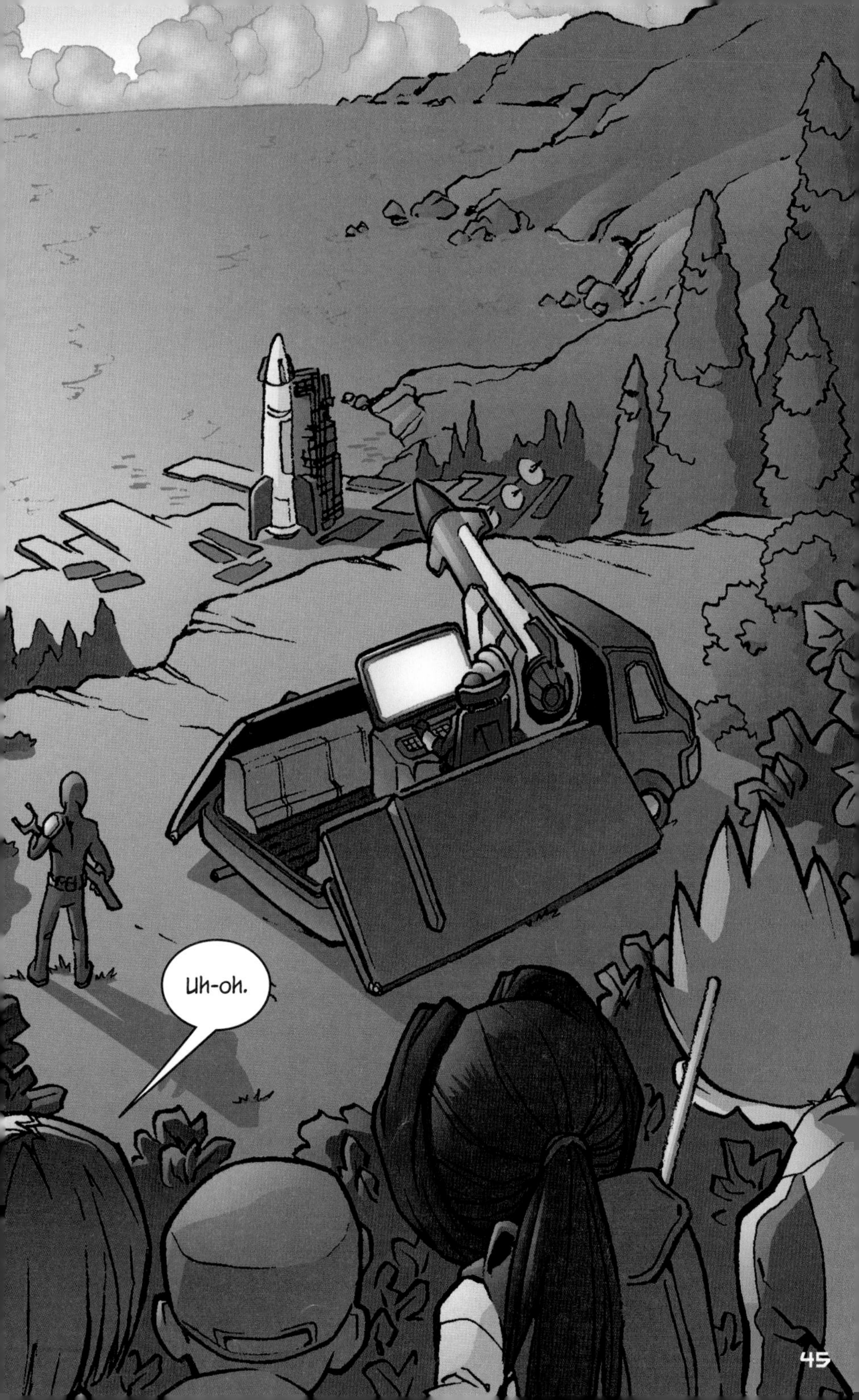
Uh-oh.

FILE NO. 1437578

SECTION 5

ACCESS GRANTED 〉〉〉〉

EMMI
MARTIAL ARTS

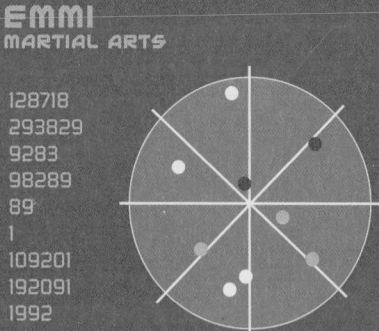

128718
293829
9283
98289
89
1
109201
192091
1992

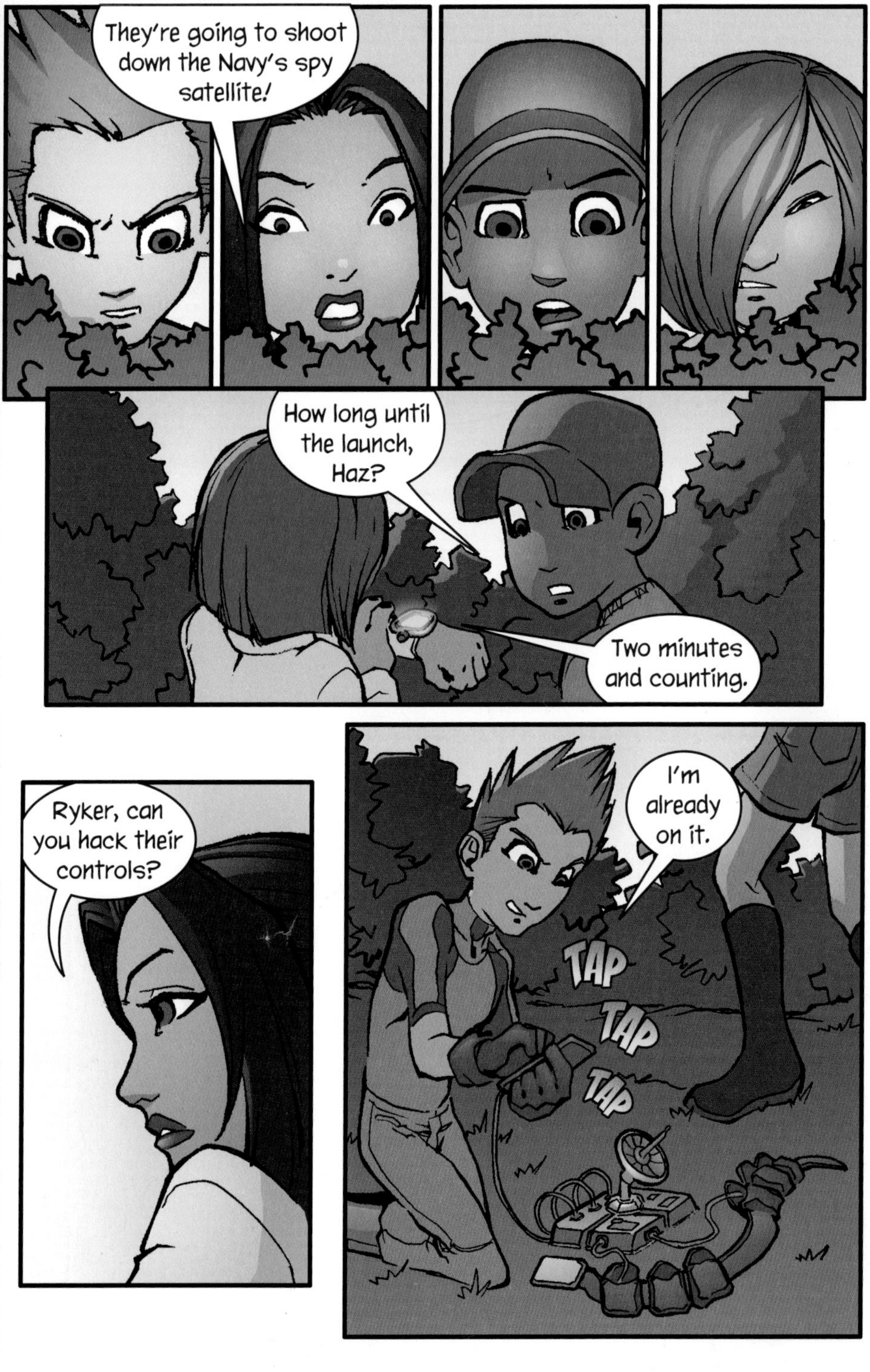
They're going to shoot down the Navy's spy satellite!
How long until the launch, Haz?
Two minutes and counting.
Ryker, can you hack their controls?
I'm already on it.
TAP
TAP
TAP

I don't have time to decrypt their code.
If I can plug into their network, I might be able to shut them down.
Jay, can you create a diversion?
I have just the thing!

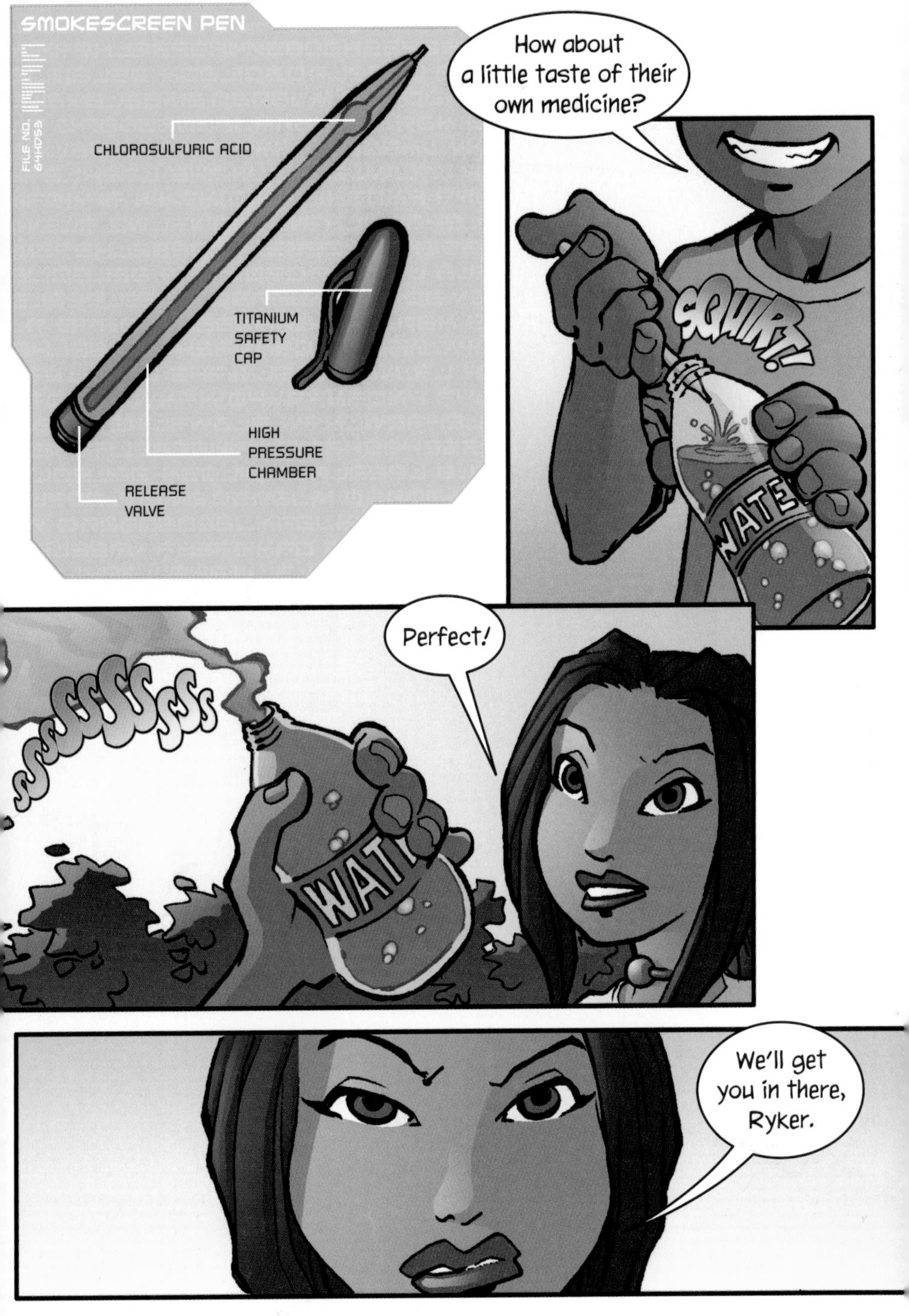
SMOKESCREEN PEN
FILE NO. 64HD53
CHLOROSULFURIC ACID
TITANIUM SAFETY CAP
HIGH PRESSURE CHAMBER
RELEASE VALVE
How about a little taste of their own medicine?
SQUIRT!
WATE
Perfect!
SSSSSSSSSSSs
WAT
We'll get you in there, Ryker.

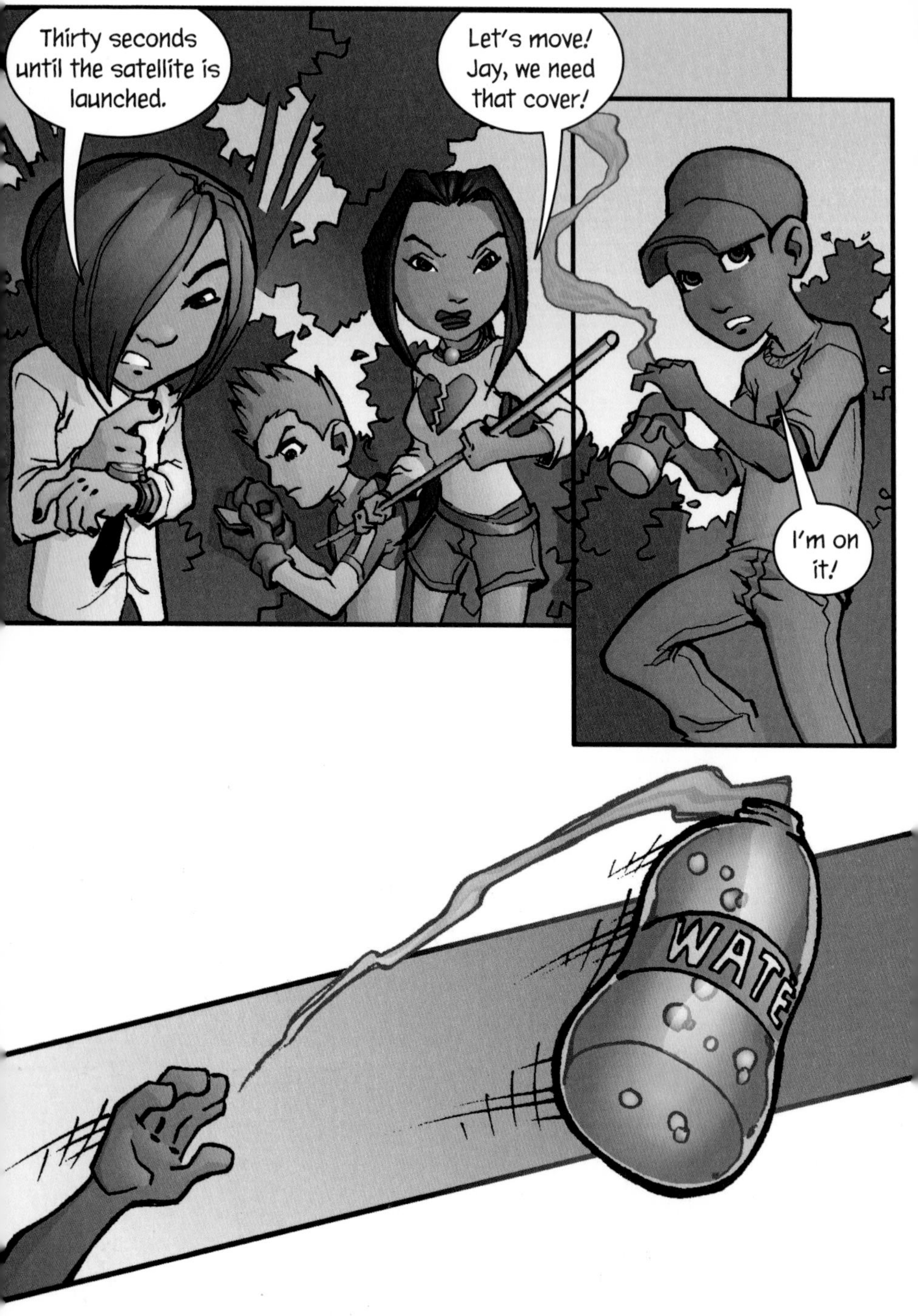
Thirty seconds until the satellite is launched.
Let's move! Jay, we need that cover!
I'm on it!
WATE

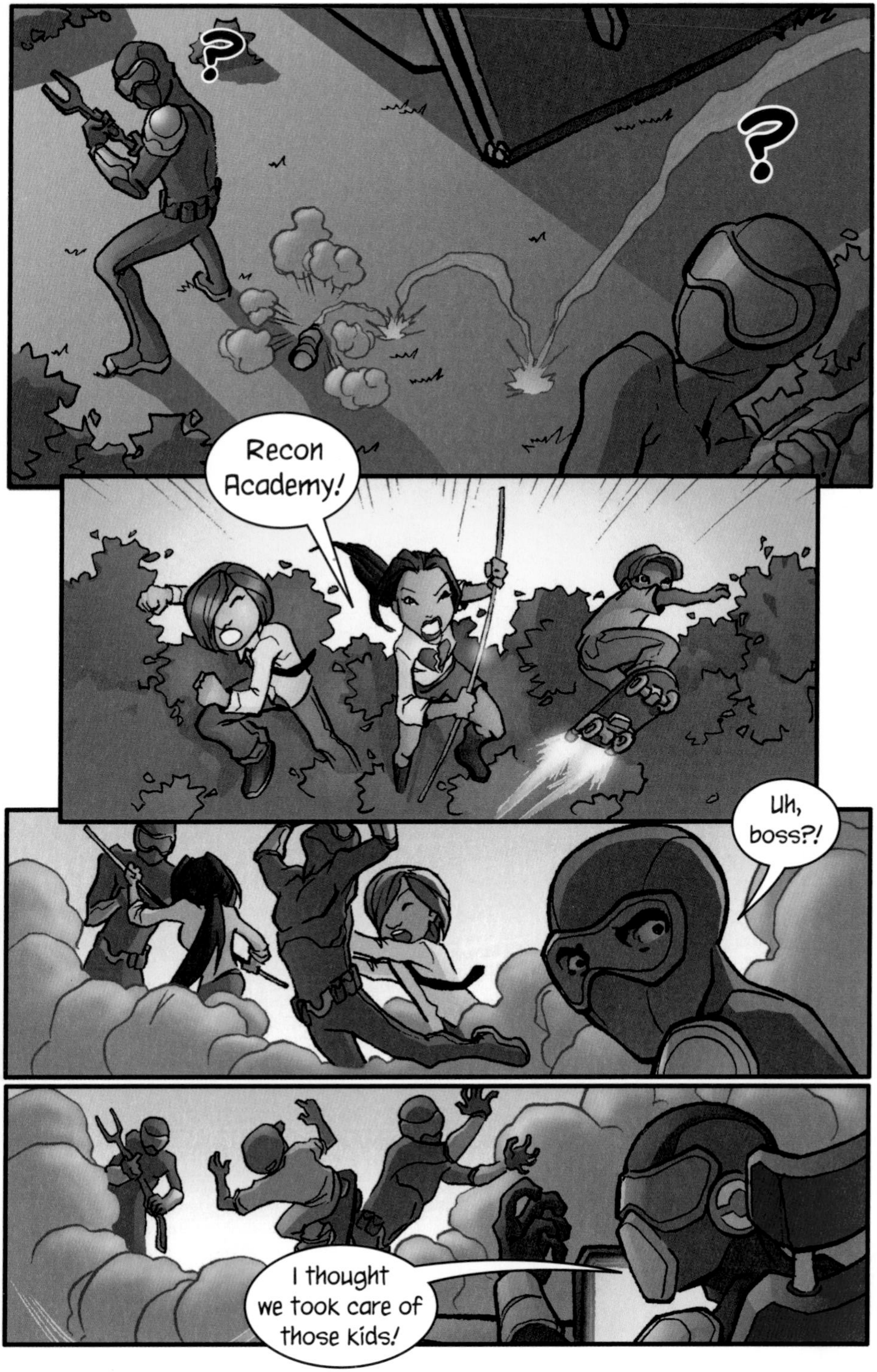
?
?
Recon Academy!
Uh, boss?!
I thought we took care of those kids!

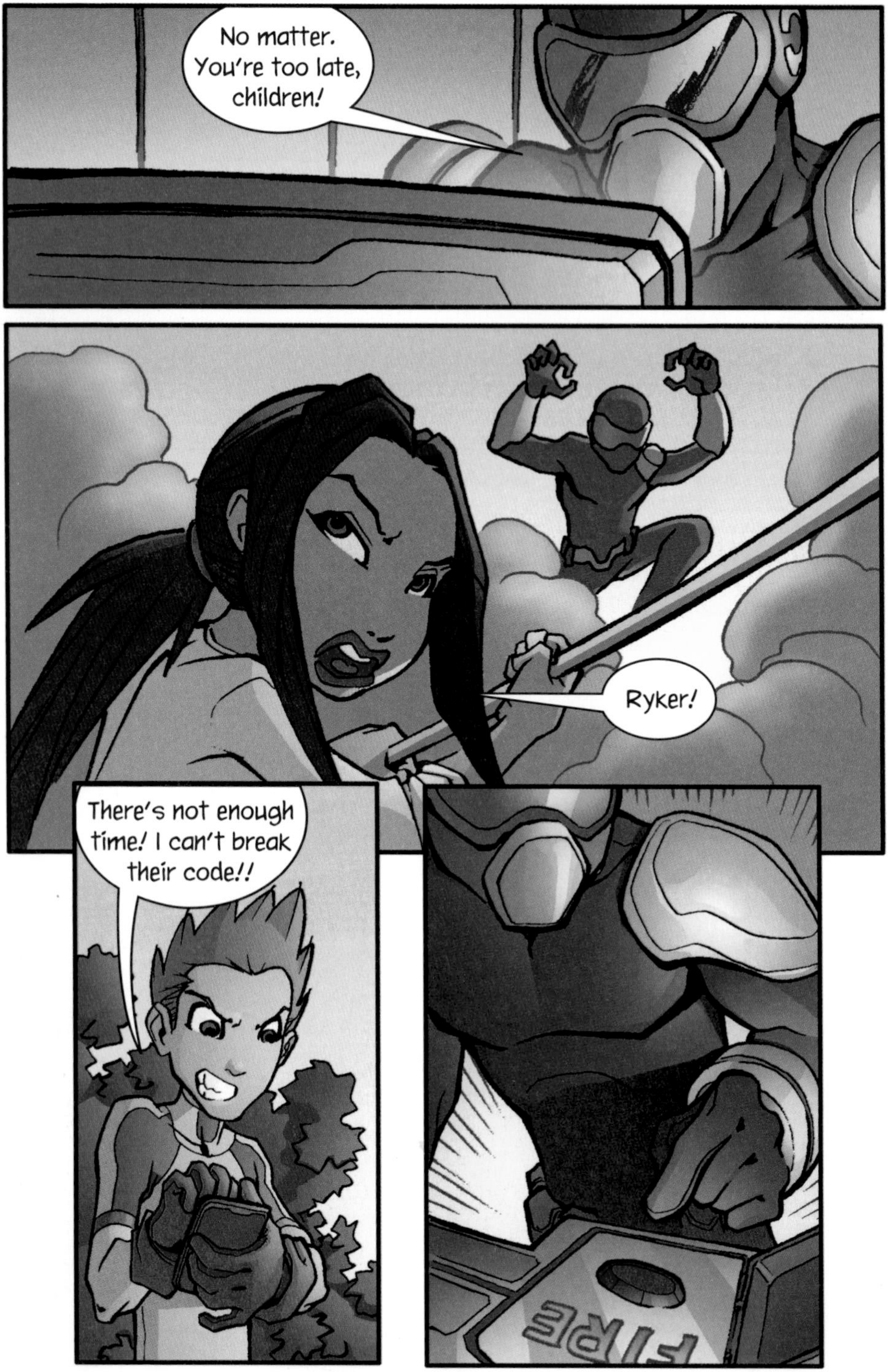
No matter. You're too late, children!
Ryker!
There's not enough time! I can't break their code!!
FIRE

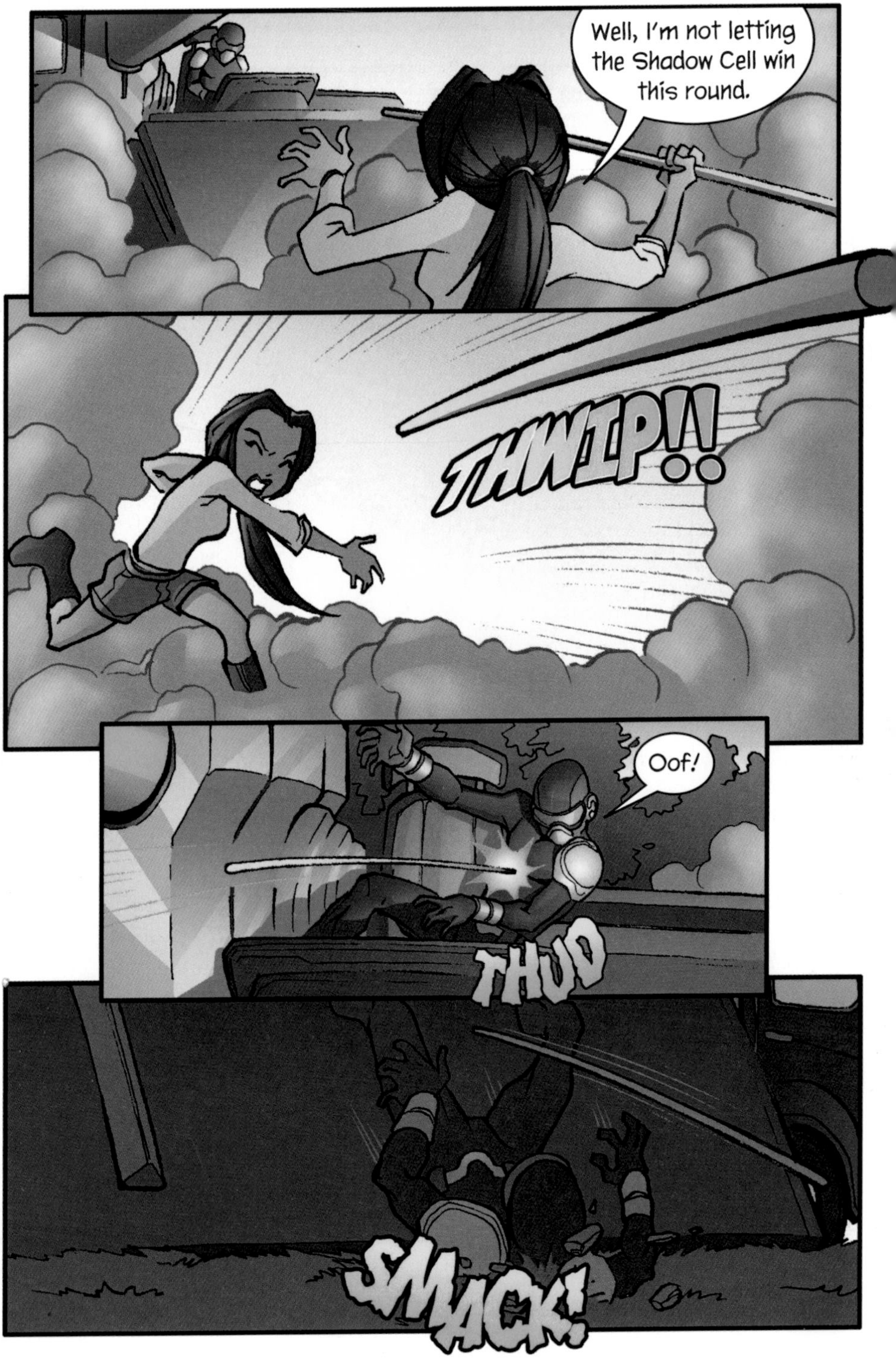
Well, I'm not letting the Shadow Cell win this round.
THWIP!!
Oof!
THUD
SMACK!

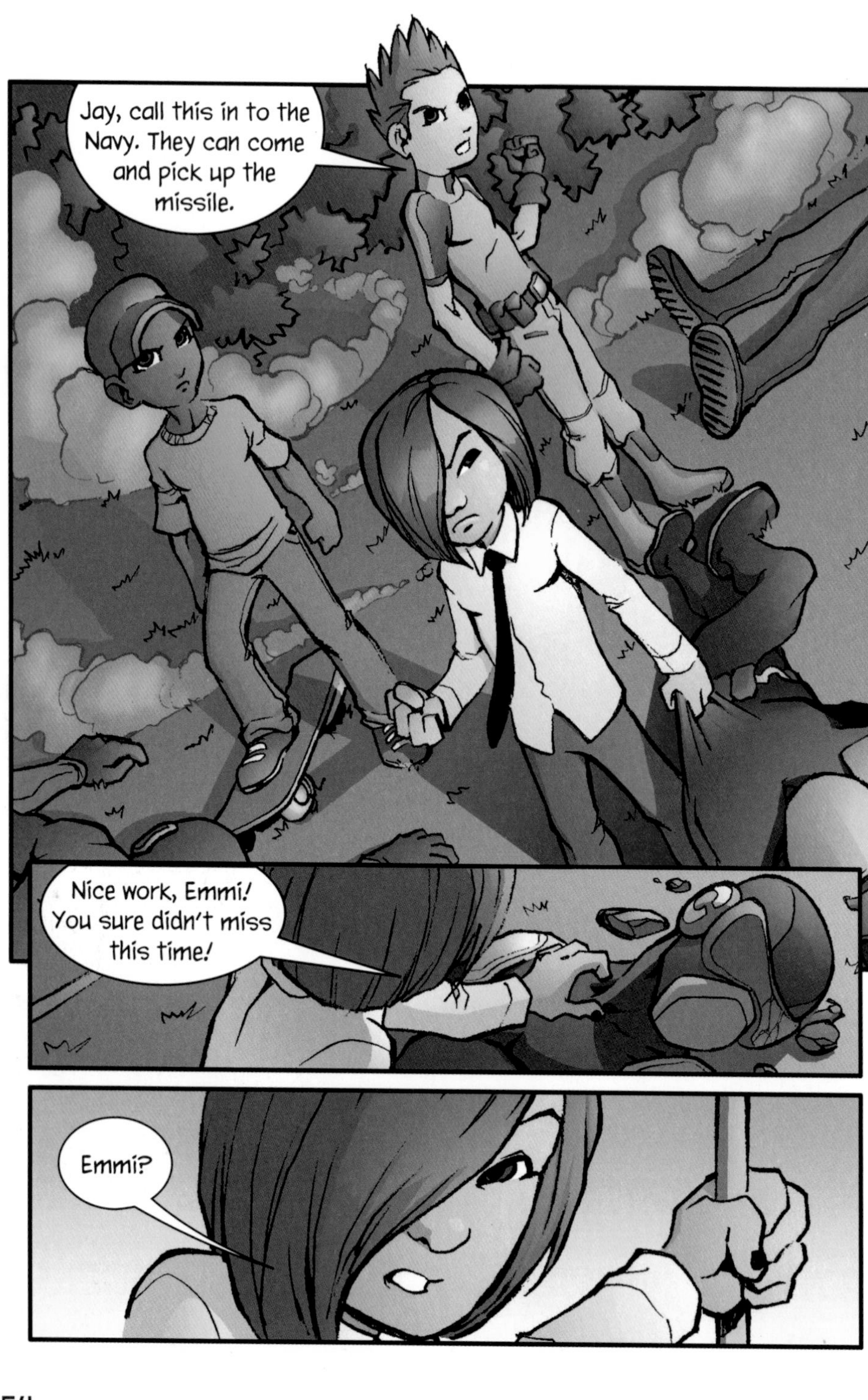
Jay, call this in to the Navy. They can come and pick up the missile.
Nice work, Emmi! You sure didn't miss this time!
Emmi?

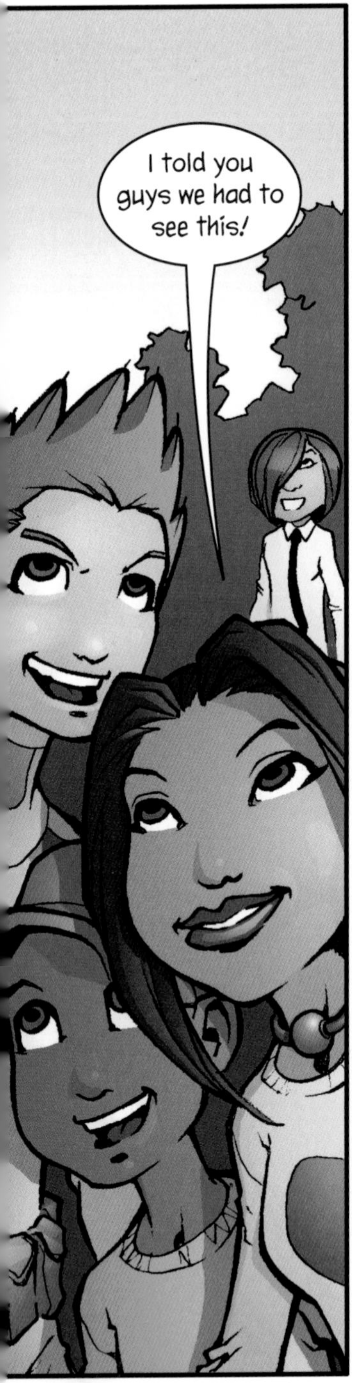
I told you guys we had to see this!

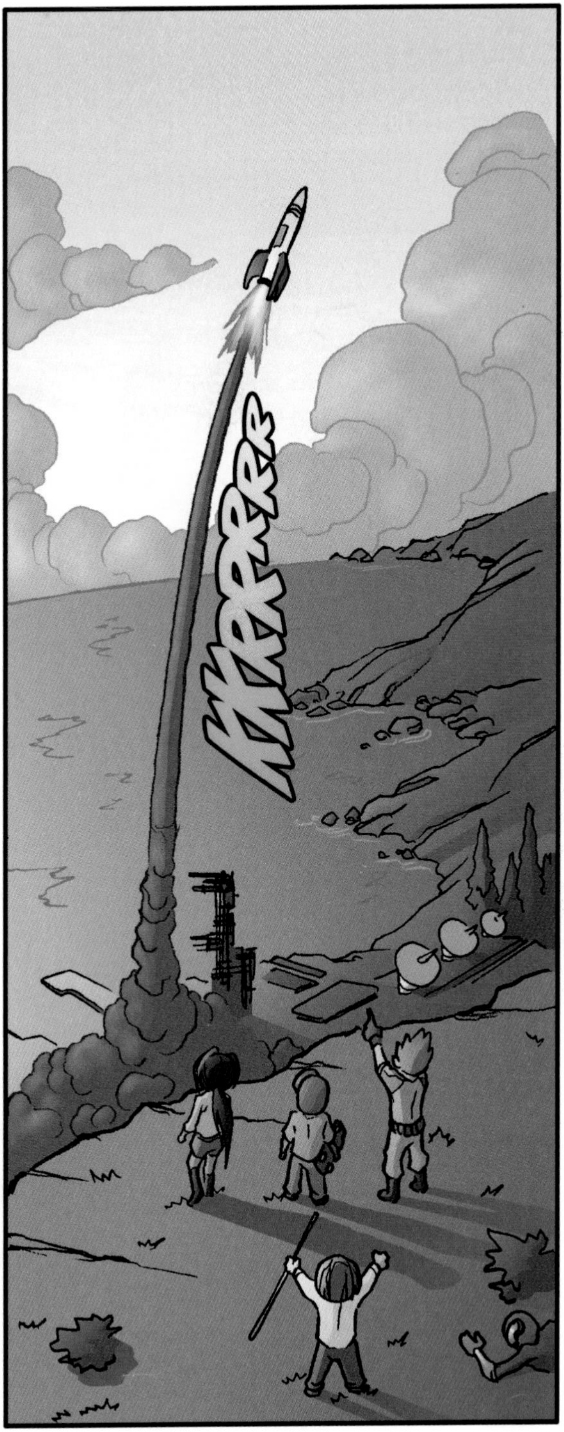
WHRRRRR

SPYSPACE

a place for international spies

PROFILE

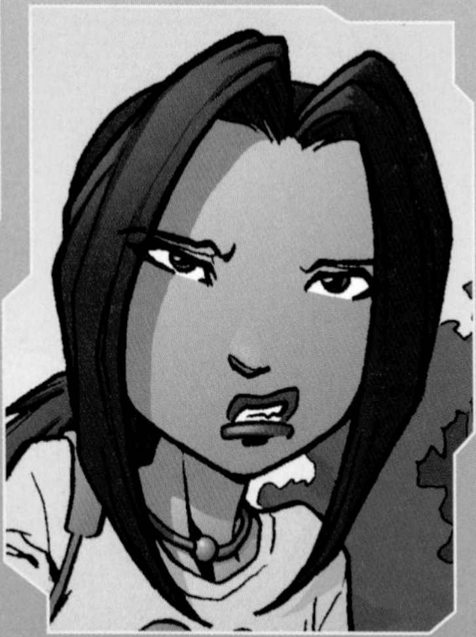

NAME: Emilia Rodriguez

CODE NAME: Emmi

AGE: 14

HEIGHT: 5' 3"

WEIGHT: 112 lbs.

EYES: Brown

HAIR: Brown

SPY ORG: Recon Academy

SPECIAL ABILITIES: Martial arts expert, gymnast, and all around great athlete (not to brag, of course)

FAVORITES: My specialized bo staff to take down enemies and perform a ton of stunts

QUOTE: "You have to believe in yourself." –Sun Tzu

PHOTOS

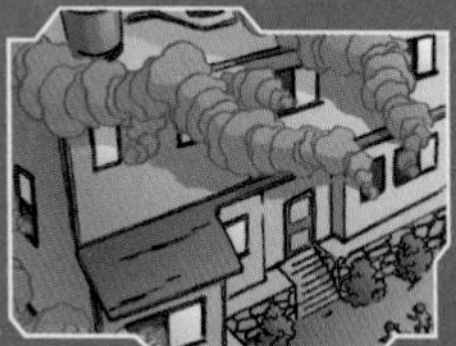

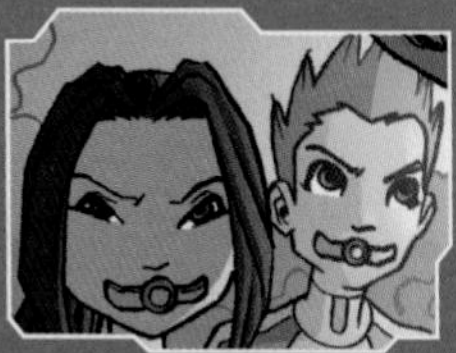

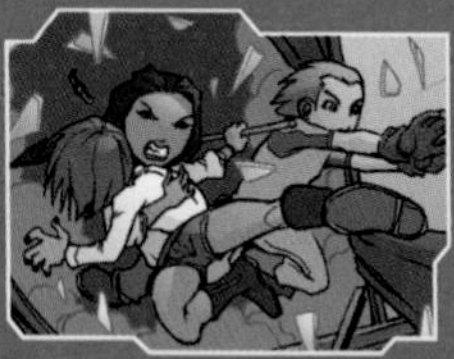

HOME SEARCH BROWSE LOGOUT

FRIENDS

Ryker Haz Jay 007

BLOG

recent posts

see all

Hey, guys! Just updated my pics and wanted to let you know that I'm back online!

Welcome back to cyberspace, Em. So, you must have gotten a new laptop.

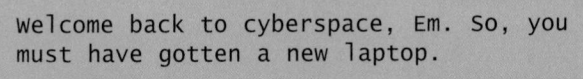

I wish :(I'm typing this message from the school library. I don't think my grandma will ever let another laptop in the house, not after what happened yesterday.

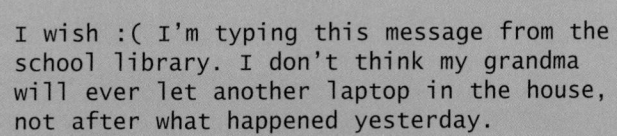

Tell me about it. My dad got so freaked, he even threw out our microwave! Plus, I'm grounded for two weeks...like blowin' up the kitchen was my fault.

Bummer.

btw, glad you guys decided to watch the launch with me. Told you it'd be totally worth it.

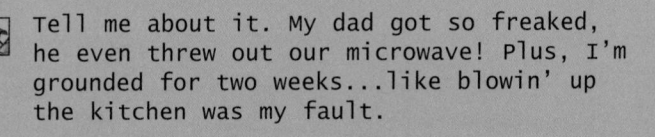

Yeah, like we had a choice ;)

⟩ CASE FILE

CASE: "Shadow Cell Scam"
CASE NUMBER: 9781434211668
AGENT: Emmi
ORGANIZATION: Recon Academy

SUSPECT: PenTech Industries

OVERVIEW: This small division of the Shadow Cell gang makes their living as highly-skilled con artists. Even the most respected agents have been fooled by their deadly trickery and get-rich-quick schemes. Be on the lookout for men with fake mustaches and terrible disguises.

CRIMINAL RECORD:
Fraud
Grand theft
Identity theft
Armed robbery

INTELLIGENCE:

anonymity (an-uh-NIM-i-tee)—the state of being unidentifiable, or unknown to others

scam (SKAM)—a trick or a lie meant to fool someone else

scheme (SKEEM)—a secret or devious plan used to take advantage of the innocent

HISTORY:

Con artists, or confidence men, rely on trust and deception to trick innocent people out of their money or possessions.

The phrase "confidence man" was first used in reference to William Thompson in 1849. Thompson went up to strangers on the street and struck up conversations with them. When he felt he had gained their trust, or confidence, he would ask to see the person's watch for a moment. After the valuable was in his hand, he would simply walk away without returning the item.

- Other names for a confidence trick: bunko, flim flam, gaffle, grift, scam, scheme, and swindle

- The person targeted by a con man is called a mark

- A con man's helpers are called shills

CONCLUSION:

In the modern world, con artists use cyberspace to scam others out of their hard-earned cash by abusing the anonymity offered by the Internet. Only the Recon Academy can safeguard us from these digital cons.

〉ABOUT THE AUTHOR

Chris Everheart always dreamed of interesting places, fascinating people, and exciting adventures. He is still a dreamer. He enjoys writing thrilling stories about young heroes who live in a world that doesn't always understand them. Chris lives in Minneapolis, Minnesota, with his family. He plans to travel to every continent on the globe, see interesting places, meet fascinating people, and have exciting adventures.

〉ABOUT THE ILLUSTRATOR

Arcana Studios, Inc. was founded by Sean O'Reilly in Coquitlam, British Columbia, in 2004. Four years later, Arcana has established itself as Canada's largest comic book and graphic novel publisher with over 100 comics and 9 books released. A nomination for a Harvey Award and winning the "Schuster Award for Top Publisher" are just a few of Arcana's accolades. The studio is known as a quality publisher for independent comic books and graphic novels.

) GLOSSARY

bogies (BOH-geez)—unidentified enemies

booted (BOO-tid)—the process of starting or restarting a computer

decrypt (dee-KRIPT)—decode or decipher

detection (di-TEK-shuhn)—the act of finding something

diversion (di-VUR-zhuhn)—an attempt to distract the enemy

hack (HAK)—gain access to computer information illegally

network (NET-wurk)—computers that are connected so they can work together.

prototype (PROH-toh-tipe)—the first version of an invention that tests an idea to see if it will work

) DISCUSSION QUESTIONS

1. Each member of Recon Academy has a special skill. Which character's skill do you think is most important when it comes to stopping Shadow Cell's evil schemes? Why?

2. If your friend was trapped in a burning building, what would you do first? What would be the safest way of handling the situation? If Jay didn't have those micro air filters, should they still have gone inside by themselves?

3. Which one of the Recon team members do you like the most? Why?

) WRITING PROMPTS

1. Emmi uses her martial arts and gymnastics skills to fight crime. Make a list of examples where Emmi uses her special skills to get out of sticky situations.

2. On page 11, Hazmat discovers that Shadow Cell has stolen some laptops. What was Shadow Cell planning to do with them? Describe their evil plan.

3. Pretend you're the newest member of Recon Academy. Draw a picture of yourself as a character. Underneath your picture, list a few of your special skills and how they would help the team.

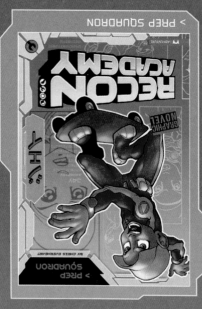
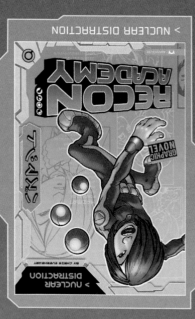
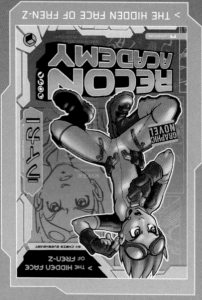

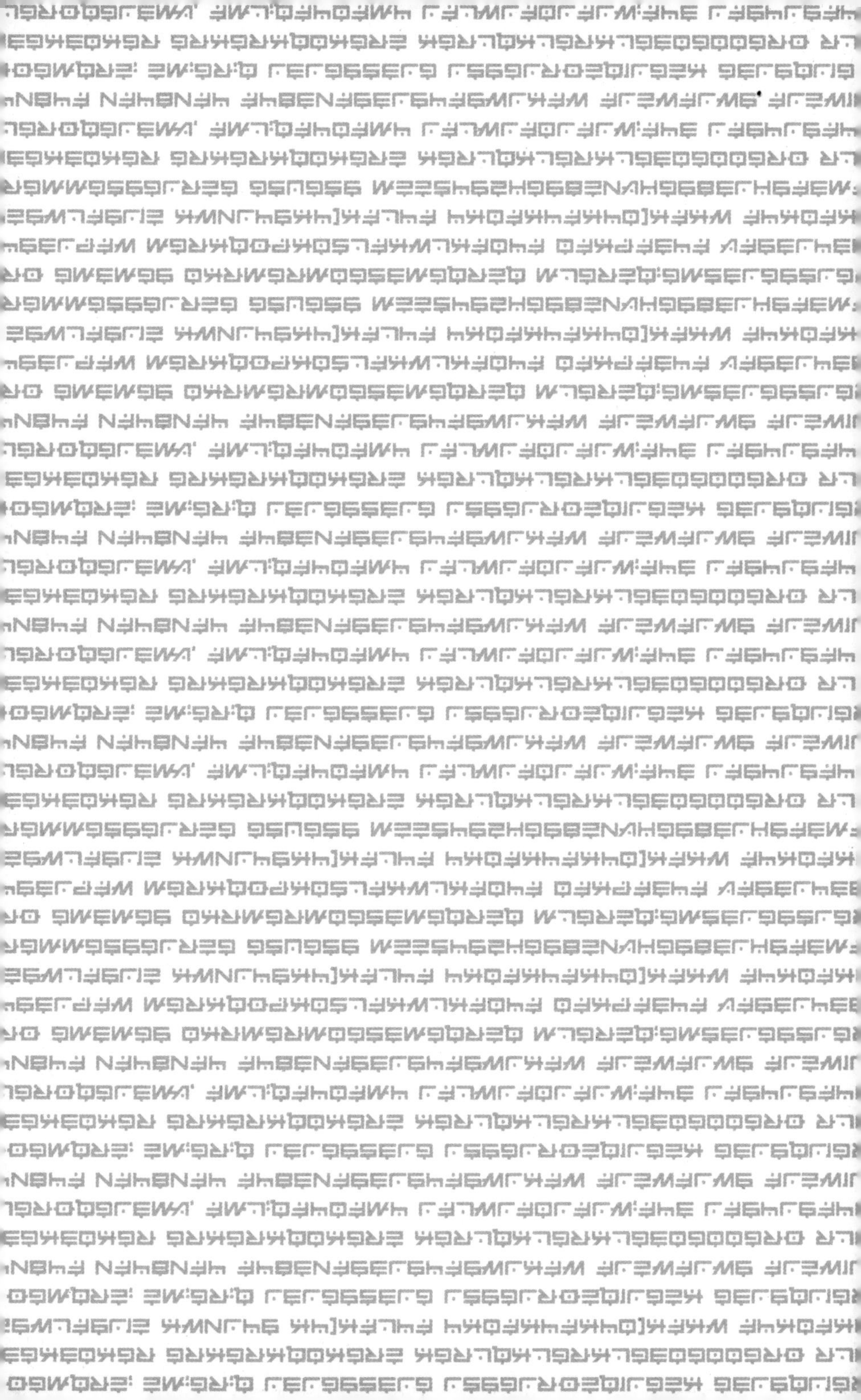

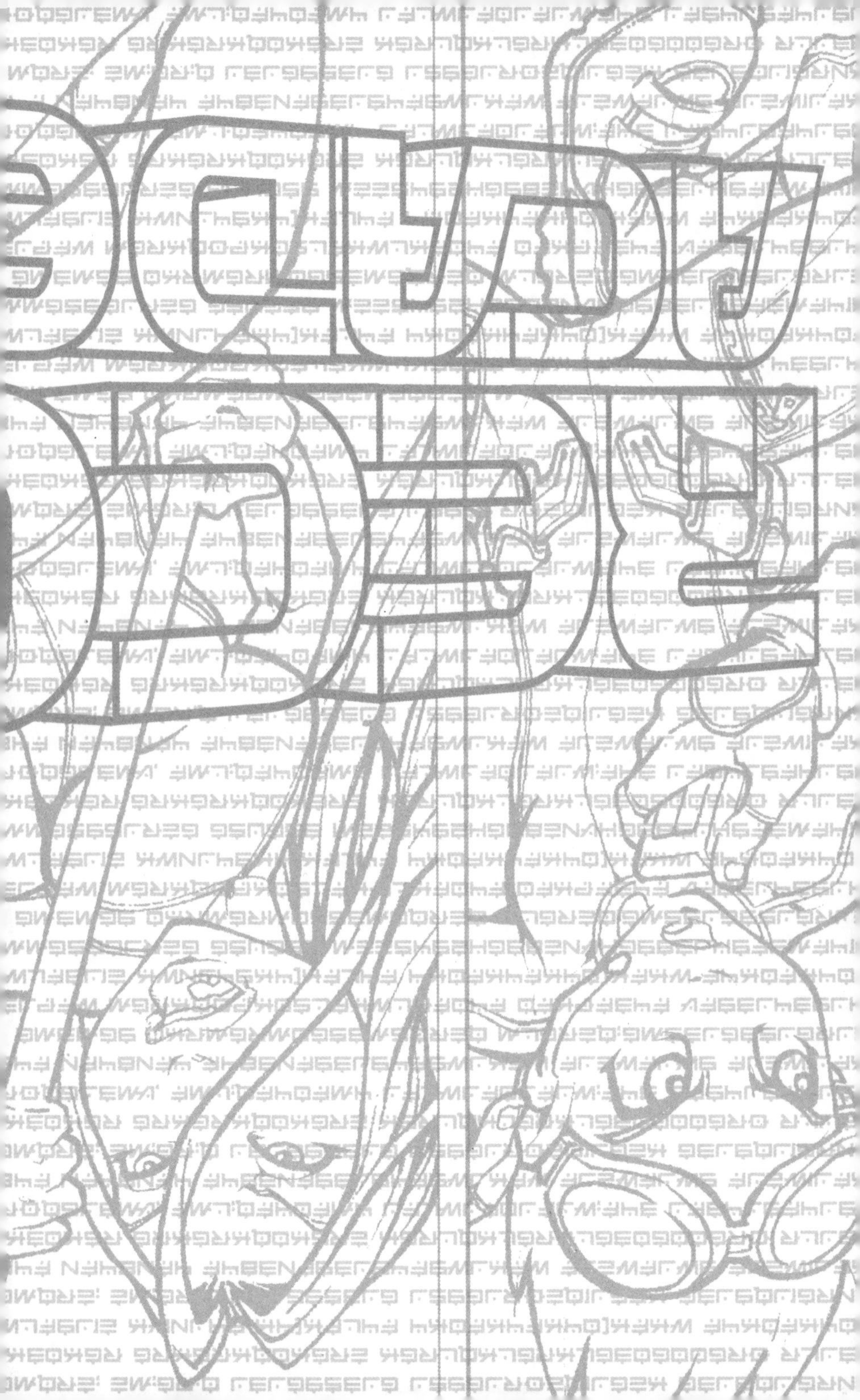